"If you need an ear, Danica said.

"I appreciate that." Ford opened the door, the pink-and-orange setting sun so beautiful in the distance.

She didn't want to go. She wanted to give him privacy with his thoughts, but she would have to force herself out the door. "Well, bye."

"I'll text you about another matchmaking night," he said and then suddenly reached out his hand.

She took it and then wrapped her arms around him and he pulled her close.

Danica closed her eyes, reveling in the feel of him against her, his strong chest, the scent of his soap and shampoo. She glanced up at him, and he touched her face and then suddenly they were kissing, his arms tightening around her, one hand winding its way into her hair. Her legs were all wobbly.

"I didn't intend on that," he said. But he didn't step back.

"Me, either." *And I want more.*

Dear Reader,

Women are scarce in Bear Ridge, Wyoming, and the cowboys are lonesome. So the tiny town recruits single ladies of all ages. Police chief Ford Dawson was looking to settle down and start a family of his own, but after what happened a couple months back with Danica Dunbar, he's not planning to date anytime soon. (And yes, the Danica Dunbar whom you met in my February 2021 Special Edition title, *Wyoming Cinderella*!)

Turns out that Danica has a secret she's not ready to share. But when she finds herself paired with Ford to run the town's matchmaking service, putting hopeful singles together, Danica learns a lot about what makes love and romance work. But will she and the last single Dawson sibling ever join the happy couples of Bear Ridge?

I hope you enjoy Ford and Danica's story. Feel free to write me with any comments or questions at MelissaSenate@yahoo.com and visit my website, melissasenate.com, for more info about me and my books. For lots of photos of my cat and dog, friend me over on Facebook: Facebook.com/MelissaSenate.

Happy reading!

Melissa Senate

Wyoming Matchmaker

MELISSA SENATE

HARLEQUIN

SPECIAL
EDITION

HARLEQUIN®
SPECIAL EDITION™

Recycling programs
for this product may
not exist in your area.

ISBN-13: 978-1-335-40478-7

Wyoming Matchmaker

Copyright © 2021 by Melissa Senate

This edition published by arrangement with Harlequin Books S.A.

For questions and comments about the quality of this book, please contact us at CustomerService@Harlequin.com.

Harlequin Enterprises ULC
22 Adelaide St. West, 40th Floor
Toronto, Ontario M5H 4E3, Canada
www.Harlequin.com

Printed in U.S.A.

Melissa Senate has written many novels for Harlequin and other publishers, including her debut, *See Jane Date*, which was made into a TV movie. She also wrote seven books for Harlequin Special Edition under the pen name Meg Maxwell. Her novels have been published in over twenty-five countries. Melissa lives on the coast of Maine with her teenage son; their rescue shepherd mix, Flash; and a lap cat named Cleo. For more information, please visit her website, melissasenate.com.

Books by Melissa Senate

Harlequin Special Edition

Dawson Family Ranch

For the Twins' Sake
Wyoming Special Delivery
A Family for a Week
The Long Awaited Christmas Wish
Wyoming Matchmaker

Montana Mavericks: What Happened to Beatrix?

The Cowboy's Comeback

Montana Mavericks: Six Brides for Six Brothers

Rust Creek Falls Cinderella

Montana Mavericks: The Lonelyhearts Ranch

The Maverick's Baby-in-Waiting

Visit the Author Profile page
at Harlequin.com for more titles.

Chapter One

Detective Ford Dawson's latest case: a missing wedding gown. With one unexpected twist.

"So you came home from work and your dress was gone?" Ford asked Trudy Dunbar, the middle-aged woman sitting across from him on the sofa. He tried hard to keep from looking at the younger woman—the aforementioned twist—sitting beside the victim.

He'd taken note of the surname when Trudy had called the Bear Ridge Police Department to report the theft, but he hadn't expected her to be necessarily related to Danica Dunbar—or that Danica would be here with Trudy. Luckily for Ford, he had a solid poker face, which had helped to hide the jolt he'd felt at the sight of her. He could easily see the family resemblance between the two women, though Trudy was probably twenty-five years older, a few inches shorter, with straight blond hair cut to her chin.

Tears brimmed in Trudy's hazel eyes. "Well, I got home from work, changed into comfortable clothes and then took Bixby for a walk—that's my French bulldog."

At his name, the little black-and-white dog scampered over, jumped up on the sofa and settled beside Trudy.

"The dress was there when I left, hanging on a hook on the back of my bedroom door," Trudy added. "When I returned, it was gone."

"How long were you out?" he asked.

"About forty-five minutes. I take Bixby to the park every night at six thirty. It's our routine."

A routine someone had obviously noticed.

"My niece here bought me the dress as a wedding gift," Trudy said, looking at Danica with tear-filled eyes. "So I feel doubly terrible that it was stolen. I just brought it home yesterday."

"Don't you worry, Aunt Trudy," Danica said, squeezing the older woman's hand. "Ford—

Detective Dawson," she quickly corrected, "will get your gown back and before the wedding."

And how could you possibly know that? he wanted to snap. Two months ago, they'd shared an unforgettable night together before she'd left his bed at three in the morning like it was spewing hot lava—without explanation. He could be the worst detective in Wyoming for all she knew about him.

He wasn't—Ford was damned good at his job. But still. Danica hadn't had a chance to get to know him. So what had sent her running out of his life so fast? After a night that couldn't have gone any better—until it had come to a screeching halt. He was a seasoned detective and couldn't figure this out. It grated.

"Do you have any idea who might have taken the dress?" he asked, flipping a page in his notebook. This wasn't a typical burglary; nothing else had been taken or disturbed. He doubted someone randomly broke in, noticed the wedding gown hanging on the back of the bedroom door, and decided to make off with only it instead of the contents of Trudy's jewelry box, which according to Trudy included an untouched diamond tennis bracelet. Someone had targeted the gown itself.

Trudy took a sip of her coffee. "Well, my fiancé was dating three different women before we met, and they do all give me the stink-eye when they see me around." She shrugged. "Two of them marched up to Cole to yell at him when I was standing right next to him."

Hmm. A jealous ex? Could be.

"Do you know their names?" Ford asked.

Trudy shook her head. "You'd have to ask Cole, though I'm not sure he'd feel comfortable telling you. He probably wouldn't want to accuse anyone without proof. Cole is such a tenderhearted man."

A month ago, Ford might not have thought that a man dating four women at the same time could be described as tenderhearted. But such was the new normal in town, ever since almost one hundred single women of all ages had moved to Bear Ridge, ready to pair up with their soul mates. There'd been a severe shortage of single women—ten men to every woman—and it had started affecting more than just lonely bachelors. The few restaurants and bars had begun to fail. The one bridal shop closed. Young people were leaving in droves for Prairie City, a bigger, more bustling town a half hour away. Business at the Dawson Family Guest Ranch, which Ford co-owned with his five siblings, was booming since the majority of their guests were from out of town and state. But two good cowboys and a reliable cook in the cafeteria had quit, saying they were moving on since there was no nightlife anymore, no one to ask out. The one single cowgirl on staff, hounded for dates day and night, couldn't take it another second and quit. She'd moved to Prairie City.

That had led the new mayor and town council, which included Ford's sister, Daisy, to hatch a plan to bring single women to town to boost the economy and keep folks here. After a social media blitz about Bear Ridge's available and marriage-minded men—there'd been an accompanying photo of a wealthy rancher who looked a lot like one of the Marvel movie actors—the women had started coming to town in droves to meet their potential true loves. A free matchmaking service was provided, too.

Ford, who was looking to settle down, hadn't bothered signing up. Not after what had happened with Danica.

But dating was now the town pastime for singles. The bars and restaurants and parks and Main Street were full of couples, full of dates and even wedding ceremonies after whirlwind romances. At a speed dating event a few weeks ago that Ford had worked—there was always at least one fistfight at this kind of thing—the mayor had announced that dating was a numbers game and sometimes you had to kiss a lot of frogs to find your prince or princess. The singles had taken that to heart and you'd see the same man or woman with a new date every day until a match was made. But that didn't mean feelings didn't get hurt.

Love was serious business. Everyone knew that.

"I'm sorry about your gown, Ms. Dunbar, and I will do my best to get it back for you," Ford said to Trudy. "I'll be in touch the moment I have information for you." He took a final sip of his coffee and then stood. "Oh, when is the wedding?"

"In two weeks—on Saturday night," Danica said. She popped up. "I'll walk you out."

Interesting. Maybe he'd finally get his explanation for what happened back in February. But should he be thinking about that two months later? Harping on it? Completely down on dating when there were plenty of single women in Bear Ridge now?

"I sure hope Aunt Trudy doesn't leave town because of this," Danica whispered as she walked him out to the porch. "She moved here for a fresh start and now that she's found her second chance at love, this might taint it and send her and her fiancé packing."

He remembered Danica talking about her lack of family in town during their night together. Her parents had retired to Arizona and her one sibling lived far away, so she'd been alone here. Her aunt Trudy, one of her few remaining relatives, had been married to a man who hated small-town life, but they'd divorced recently and Trudy had finally come back to her hometown.

Ford had once felt the same as Trudy's ex. It had taken him a long time to realize it wasn't small-town life he had a problem with, but the particular small town of Bear Ridge. The minute Ford had graduated from high school, he'd fled. Leaving his five siblings behind hadn't been easy, but staying was out of the question back then. He'd moved to Casper, a small city hours away, and become a cop. But the life he'd built there had been missing something for a long time. It had taken him almost twenty years to come home.

Now he was the last single Dawson. One by one, his siblings had moved back to the Dawson Family Guest Ranch, where they'd all once said they'd never step foot again. And one by one, they'd met their matches in every context. Then there was him. The oldest, at thirty-five—and alone.

And now that Bear Ridge was full of single women, he was hung up on the one who'd walked away. Same old story.

He looked at Danica, beautiful in the glow of

the porch light, her long blond hair in a swirly tumble past her shoulders, her blue eyes full of so many different emotions he couldn't assess them all. He saw worry for her aunt. And clear nervousness about standing here with him. Yeah, he wasn't too comfortable either. From naked in his bed to awkward almost-strangers.

"I promise you I'll do my best to find the thief and the dress," he said. He couldn't promise it would be in one piece or that it wasn't in an alleyway Dumpster, covered in garbage. He'd seen the damage inflicted by scorned exes, and it was never pretty.

"I appreciate that," she said. "Especially given—" She clamped her mouth shut.

Especially given what happened between us... how awkward this is...

"No worries," he said.

But he didn't mean it. How was he supposed to move on from Danica when he didn't know what had gone wrong between them? They'd made love, fed each other whipped-cream-covered strawberries, then lay spooned and talked about everything and anything for hours. He'd been so relaxed with her against his chest, his arms wrapped around her. He'd been hopeful about the newfangled future he envisioned for himself. And then she'd crept off in the middle of the night, mumbling something about how this wasn't going to work, sorry, but she had to go. The next day he'd left her a voice mail: no response. He'd sent roses to her office, asking if they could talk. All he'd gotten back was a two-line text saying they just weren't a match, sorry.

He'd been so damned thrown for a loop that he'd considered asking his sister, whose favorite subject was relationships, what the hell could have gone wrong, but he couldn't bring himself to talk about it. He just grumbled around for a few weeks. And now he was once again close enough to Danica Dunbar to smell her intoxicating perfume.

"I'll be in touch with your aunt," he said, emphasizing the words *your aunt*.

She nodded and he booked down the stairs and into his squad car.

He'd spent all those weeks trying to forget her, and now he was right back into remembering.

Danica stayed out on the porch, needing to catch her breath and slow her heart rate. When her aunt had called the Bear Ridge Police Department about the burglary, Danica had figured there was only a small chance of Ford Dawson being the cop to show up. But, lately, the odds hadn't been in Danica's favor in any aspect of her life.

"He sure was a handsome one."

Danica turned around to find her aunt coming outside.

So handsome. Six feet two, rock-hard muscles, thick dark hair and the bluest eyes. The way he kissed… "Yeah, I guess," Danica said, trying for a neutral expression. "I'm sure he'll find your dress, Aunt Trudy. Ford is very dedicated to his job and this community."

Trudy narrowed her eyes. "Ford, huh? You clearly know him. I thought I sensed something in the air. You two have a history?"

Danica nodded and leaned against the porch railing. "Unfortunately, we…want different things," she said as memories of lying in his arms came flooding back. "I think I should just be on my own for a while. Till I figure myself out."

"You do what feels right," her aunt said, putting an arm around her.

That made Danica feel better. Though she wasn't sure what *was* right. After her marriage had fallen apart a year ago, she'd taken that entire time for herself, to regroup, to cry, to know who she was apart from her ex, a man she'd been with since middle school. Before the influx of single women, Danica had been asked out constantly. She'd finally started saying yes to the ones who seemed kind. She hadn't connected with anyone. Until Ford.

For a few beautiful hours back in February, she thought she'd found the man of her dreams in Ford Dawson. Kind. Honest. Open. Warm. Funny. Generous. So good-looking. Seriously sexy. And what a kisser. The moment she'd felt his lips against hers, she'd been a goner.

And then, as they lay together in bed, her back against his chest, his arms around her, he'd mentioned children, and anxiety had pushed the air out of her. He hoped for six, like his parents had had. At least four, for sure. Any combination.

Danica was thirty-one and had yet to feel maternal urges, that stirring her friends talked about. She loved children, particularly her goddaughter, her best friend Molly's one-year-old baby girl. But her ex-husband, who'd left her after ten years of marriage because she hadn't been ready to start a family, had told her he didn't think she'd ever be ready and she should just admit the truth—that she didn't want a child. Danica didn't think that was true. She'd always been able to see herself with a baby—way in the future. But the want, the maternal feelings, the baby fever, even during the early years of her marriage when she'd thought she was finally on her way to being happy, feeling safe and secure in the world, never happened.

She'd lost her marriage because of I'm-just-not-ready. And she hadn't been able to talk about it with anyone, not even her best friend. When Danica's ex had confessed to cheating on her, to having fallen for someone else, Molly had been newly pregnant, going through her own divorce, and Danica hadn't felt comfortable talking about her lack of baby fever. Recently Danica had finally told Molly that she wasn't sure she wanted kids, and her friend's theory made her feel better about not being ready.

According to Molly, Danica's ex-husband was the typical golden boy who liked trophies, which Danica always had been to him until she wouldn't give him what he wanted next: a child. So he'd left her. Molly truly believed that Danica had married him more because it had been expected and was safe than because there was any great love between them. She thought that when Danica did fall in love, as an adult woman with experience behind her, she just might feel those first maternal urges.

Maybe to all of it. Maybe not. There was nothing wrong with not wanting children.

But there was something wrong with starting

a relationship with a man who'd made it crystal clear he wanted *six* kids.

So she'd made excuses and fled the house that she herself had found for Ford as his real estate agent. He'd had a housewarming party earlier that day, and she hadn't left until three in the morning.

"Well, I'm gonna head upstairs and pack," Trudy said. "Good thing I only rented this Airbnb till the end of the month."

Danica nodded, turning to head back into the cute little house. Many married residents and retirees had listed their homes on the vacation rental websites and were raking it in while taking long-awaited vacations, the singles having long filled up the few inns in town and the motels just outside of town. She'd invited Trudy to stay with her, but her aunt had wanted her own space and somewhere to "canoodle" with her dates. Not feeling comfortable staying in the rental anymore, Trudy was moving in with her fiancé and both the bride and groom were excited for the jumpstart on their lives together.

"Ga-ba!"

Danica turned at the sweet little voice. Across the street, a toddler was walking between a young man and woman, each holding a hand. Every few steps, they'd swing her forward, giggles bursting.

Danica smiled, waiting for that feeling to come over her. The *I want that*. It didn't.

"Ooh, Danica! Danica!"

Danica looked across the street to see the mayor of Bear Ridge waving at her and rushing toward her. What was this about?

"I'm hoping you can help me," Pauline Abbott said, pushing her square silver glasses up on her nose. "I'm fresh out of a meeting and it seems the team working on a round of matchmaking applications was doing a terrible job. You know everyone in town, Danica. And since you're not dating, would you help?"

Danica was about to wonder how the mayor knew so much about her personal life, and then remembered that Pauline had been sitting at the next table in Grill 307 yesterday when Danica had been having lunch with Molly and grumbled, "Ugh, I'm not dating anymore, that's it. Mr. Right will just have to drop out of the sky."

That was basically how Molly had ended up with her own dream man. She'd pretty much just had to wait until Zeke Dawson, one of Ford's brothers, got over himself, and once he did, he realized the woman he'd been looking for was right there all along. Molly, his administrative assistant, and now a partner in business and life.

"It's not done by computer and algorithms?" Danica asked.

"Goodness, no," Pauline said. "Matching ticked boxes isn't going to bring people together. Oh, whoop-de-do, they both like horses and walking along the beach at sunset." She let out one of her famous snorts. "Our system takes a bit longer, but our matchmakers can pair people based on real compatibility—what they actually say they want in a partner."

Makes sense, Danica thought. "What do I need to do?" she asked. "Seems like a lot of responsibility. A lot to get wrong. Like the predecessor did."

Pauline waved a hand. "Oh, you'll do wonders. You're in the business of bringing people and houses together. It's the same concept, only it's people and people. You just match folks up with what they're really looking for. Someone says they want three bedrooms and two baths, you don't show them two-bedrooms-and-one-bath properties, right?"

"Right," Danica agreed. Huh. "I suppose I could give it a go." Maybe she'd find a great guy whose paternal urges weren't stirring past the age of thirty, either.

"You're a peach!" Mayor Abbott said, handing Danica the forms. "There are about fifty-some-odd here. Our motto at Bear Ridge Matchmaking Central—a lid for every pot. Of course, not everyone in this group will be a match, but there's more where this came from every day as singles put themselves back in after bad dates. We do have a good success rate, though."

That had to be true, based on all the handholding going on in town, plus Danica's own aunt. Even Danica's neighbor three houses down, a sweet widower with four very yippy but cute dogs, had found love with a woman with two huge Irish wolfhounds and two cats. They were going to make it work.

The mayor zipped back across to her car and drove off.

Danica stared at the pile of wants and hopes and dreams in her hand. How wonderful would it be to bring people together, bring love into their lives, even if she had to be alone.

Chapter Two

Ford had a half hour left on his shift, so he headed over to Cole Harmon's house, not too far from the center of town. Cole was an accountant with an office on Main Street, and from the little Ford knew about him, Trudy Dunbar's fiancé was a solid citizen. He found the man outside, constructing a flower box in the front yard in the sun's last light, two border collies lying on the porch steps.

As Ford exited his squad car in the driveway, Cole walked over. "What a mess. But, as I told Trudy, I have no idea who would have taken her dress." He shook his head. "Could it really have been one of the women I was dating?"

"Well, it's somewhere to start," Ford said.

Cole let out a sigh, and Ford got it. Cole didn't want to name names when there was no proof his exes had anything to do with theft. "I went out with Samantha Withers four times."

Samantha Withers. A blond woman in her early fifties who managed the garden center came to mind. Ford had been back in Bear Ridge only a few months, but he tended to know who was who.

Ford jotted that down in his notebook. He'd use his phone's Notes app, but the old-fashioned method made it clear what he was doing, and that tended to put people at ease. People at ease talked more, opened up. "You broke up with her?"

Cole nodded. "I was very casually dating three women when I got matched with Trudy. We met and that was it. I knew she was the one in fifteen minutes. I called all three women the next day and told them I enjoyed getting to know them but I'd met the woman I was gonna marry."

Huh. "You said that?"

"I did. I was that sure. And I was right. Getting married in two weeks."

Had Ford felt that way about Danica? In the past, his mind never went to marriage; he'd been pushing away serious relationships and commitments from the get-go. But now that he did want to find his other half and have children, now that he was actually ready, a different feeling had come over Ford as he'd held Danica in his arms and they'd talked while eating those strawberries. It had been the absence of that familiar tightness in his chest, in his throat, when he'd get too close with a woman he was seeing. The warmth and contentment and ease when he'd been with Danica had settled in his chest instead. Maybe *that* was knowing? Very likely it was just the first step. But a step Ford was glad to finally be taking, even if he'd gotten his heart handed back to him.

"How'd Samantha take the breakup?" he asked.

"Not well. She ranted in my ear and told me I led her on and that she never would have gone to Horizon Point with me if she'd thought I was going to end things a couple days later."

Horizon Point was a famed overlook in Bear Ridge with a gorgeous view of the mountains and the Bear Ridge River. Lots of engagements happened there. And two murders, both so-called "crimes of passion," an old-fashioned phrase that had always bothered Ford. However, the murders were decades old and sixty-two years apart.

"And the next lady?" Ford asked.

"CeCe Womax. When I called her to tell her I'd met The One, she demanded to know who it was, if she was younger, and then yelled at me for a good minute and said I was a 'class-A jerk' and that she hoped *I* got dumped." CeCe's name didn't ring a bell. She was likely a newcomer.

Ford jotted all that down. "And the third?"

"Brianne Johnson. She was just quiet for a moment and then said, 'well, isn't that nice' and wished me well. That was it. So I doubt it was her."

Except sometimes the quiet ones made the loudest moves in secret. Brianne had her own dog-training/grooming business. He knew this because he'd once taken his brothers' dogs to her. Ford had been dog sitting, and both Dude and River had rolled in something disgusting. When a simple bath didn't get rid of the stink, he'd taken them to Brianne, who'd fit him in right away and returned them slightly lavender-scented.

The culprit could be any of them or none of them. He'd devote tomorrow morning to talking to each one. Ford had a few other cases going, but he wanted to get back Trudy's dress—if it was in one piece—as soon as humanly possible.

"Find your better half, yet?" Cole asked.

"Nah. I haven't been as lucky as you."

"You'll find her," Cole said with the assurance of a man in love.

Ford had to get the ridiculous notion out of his

head that he had *already* found her. For whatever reason, his very brief relationship with Danica Dunbar hadn't worked out, and he needed to let it go.

Danica sat at her kitchen table, a cup of coffee to her left and the pile of matchmaking requests in front of her. There were fifty-four forms, half men, half women. Each form had either been uploaded online and printed or turned in at the drop box at the town hall and included a max of three photos, a short "who I am and what I'm looking for" section and the usual boxes for age range and how important things such as political agreement and religious affiliation were. Danica read through the first one, from Kelly McDougal, forty-two, divorced, two teens in high school… *hoping to connect with a man who isn't looking for a mother or a maid. I'm a middle school teacher with a lot on my plate.*

Danica looked hard at Kelly's photo, trying to get a feel for her. She had a great combo of warmth and grit stamped on her face, curiosity and intelligence in her pretty hazel eyes. *Okay, Kelly, let's see who might be for you in this group.* Danica took another sip of her coffee and scanned the forms. Ooh, here was a good-looking forty-

four-year-old, also divorced, a mortgage broker...
am not interested in dating single mothers. Next!
Forty-seven-year-old Thomas was a comptroller
for the county, looking for a "traditionally minded
woman who enjoys catering to her man." Danica's
mother was that woman, and she and her husband
had been mostly happily married for thirty-five
years. Unfortunately, Danica's mother hadn't been
supportive of her when she and her ex had been
breaking up and had even said, *Well, can you
blame him for wanting a wife who wants a child?
I mean, really, Danica. Sometimes I don't think
I'll ever understand you.*

That had hurt. Bad. Because Danica wasn't too
sure she understood herself, either.

She took another long sip of her coffee to clear
her head and get back to finding love for Kelly.
But the doorbell rang, and Danica had a feeling it
might be the mayor, back with an armful of new
matchmaking requests.

It wasn't the mayor. It was Danica's older sister, Candace, with a baby in a pink-and-white car
seat. Candace looked exactly as she had the last
time Danica had seen her two years ago—tall and
slim, long straight blond hair past her shoulders,
the same blue eyes as her own. Candace's features
were a bit sharper than Danica's. They were just

a year apart, but they'd never been close, not even as children.

"Candace? This is a surprise—a very happy one," Danica said, her gaze going from her sister to the baby. Candace had called to let Danica know she was pregnant and then again when she'd had the baby, but she'd refused all offers of help or for Danica to come visit. Candace had moved to Los Angeles when she was eighteen and always claimed to be busy or going on auditions for commercials or walk-on roles in soaps. She hadn't had much success, and Danica had always heard the disappointment in Candace's voice the few times she'd actually answered the call.

Her sister's eyes got misty—and Candace Dunbar wasn't a crier. "Can I stay with you for a while? Till I get settled?"

Danica felt her heart actually soar. "Wait—you mean you're moving here?" She opened the door wide. "Come on in."

Candace stepped inside and closed the door. "It just didn't happen for me in LA. I barely have any savings left. And I have to think about Brandy," she said, caressing the beautiful baby girl's wispy blond curls. "She's five months old."

"She's absolutely precious," Danica said, marveling at the tiny creature. Her niece. Her dear sister's child, no matter how distant Candace had always been. "And of course you can stay with me. Did you know Aunt Trudy moved to Bear Ridge, too? She's engaged."

Candace's eyes widened. "Really? That's great. Last I heard she was getting divorced." She bit her lip. "I've been a terrible sister and niece. Wrapped up in my own world and problems. But I'd like to change that."

Danica grabbed her sister into a hug. "Let's start right now."

Candace smiled and gave Danica another hug. "I'm so relieved you're being so welcoming."

"Always, Candace," Danica said.

Her sister gave her another hug, which felt so good. "And I'll admit, an old friend sent me a link to a story about the call for single women and all the great available men in town. I've had one bad relationship after another in LA. I'm done with bad boys and Peter Pans. I want someone I can rely on. Someone who'll be a father to Brandy."

"Who *is* her father?"

Candace grimaced. "Someone who claims he's not, that he supposedly was told he can't have kids." Her eyes got teary again, and she blinked hard. "I've accepted that. I'm now ready for a fresh start. I just hope I don't make the same mistakes here."

"Well, sounds to me like you know what you want, Candace. I think you're gonna be just fine."

Her sister smiled. Brandy let out a little cry. "She's late for her nap. I have her bassinet in the SUV."

"This place has three bedrooms, and it's just me," Danica said, leading the way to the living room. "So you can take the big guest room and we can turn the smaller one into a nursery for Brandy."

Again Danica just stared at her little niece, marveling over how lovely and wondrous she was. A tiny being with her entire life ahead of her, the world to experience. She felt her heart truly give a little leap. *Because you're my niece? Because maybe we have a chance to be close, after all?*

Danica's friend Molly had said a time or two that she had a feeling Danica's lack of maternal urges were rooted in how distant her family was. Her parents weren't cold, exactly, but they weren't loving either. They were prickly and judgmental and tended to keep to themselves.

"Have you heard from Mom and Dad?" Danica asked.

"They sent me a generous check when Brandy

was born and they said they booked a flight to come see her, but they canceled, of course. This or that came up. I can't even remember the excuse."

"Well, like you said, fresh start. For you, me, Brandy and Aunt Trudy."

"I'm glad she found her guy," Candace said. "Trudy deserves to be happy after all she's been through." She looked at Danica. "You, too," Candace added warily, as if she was getting too personal with a sister she barely knew anymore.

"Me, too, is right," Danica said with a nod. "I've been trying, but it's not easy out there. In fact, I have a side job—volunteer—as one of the town's matchmakers. Let's go put Brandy down for her nap, and then you can fill out a form for yourself. I'll see if there are any matches for you in the stack I have."

"I just want nice. Dependable. Someone I can really count on to say what he means and mean what he says. You know?"

"I know. The last guy I dated was very up-front about what he wanted. It just didn't align," she added wistfully.

Candace nodded. "Sorry. Well, you'll find someone for yourself in that stack, too."

She wasn't looking anymore. And it wasn't like anyone could match up to Ford Dawson.

Chapter Three

All three of Cole Harmon's exes had alibis for the time frame of the theft of Trudy Dunbar's dress. Ford had had to tread carefully with how he'd approached each potential suspect. In the morning, after he'd fortified himself with two cups of coffee at the BRPD, he'd gone over to the home of Samantha Withers—the one who'd ranted in Cole's ear and complained about going to Horizon Point with him the night before he broke up with her—and said he was investigating a wedding dress stolen from Trudy Dunbar's home. He waited. Surprise had crossed Samantha's face, then she'd smirked. "Serves her right," Samantha had said as they'd stood in the foyer of her condo. "That's what that multi-timer Cole gets. Someone got mad enough to steal his fiancée's wedding gown. Ha, wait till my friends get a load of this." She'd let out a snort.

Ford had been a detective long enough to know that Samantha Withers wasn't his perp. Thieves were a lot cagier and didn't like to telegraph how glad they were about the bad "news" or how excited they were to share it with their besties.

CeCe Womax, who'd yelled at Cole and said he was a class-A jerk, had been on a date at a Mexican restaurant in Prairie City during the forty-five-minute window that Trudy's dress was taken.

Two down, one to go. Brianne Johnson, who'd wished Cole well. He didn't know Brianne all that much, but his gut told him the warm, friendly dog trainer wasn't a thief. Though her home *was* right around the corner from Trudy Dunbar's Airbnb. He knocked at Brianne's front door.

He heard a cheery "Coming!" and then footsteps. Brianne opened the door, her elderly grandmother, Delia Johnson, in a hot-pink tracksuit with a white headband around her forehead, behind her.

"Hi, Detective," Brianne said. "Need to make an appointment for one of your brothers' dogs?"

Before he could say a word, he noticed Brianne's grandmother slowly backing away. Nervously.

"Everything okay, ma'am?" he called over.

Brianne turned around. "Gram? What's wrong? You're white as a ghost."

Delia's shoulders slumped, and she held out her arms in front of her, wrists together. "The officer is here for me."

"What?" Brianne asked, confusion in her eyes.

Ah. Suddenly things were making sense.

"Oh, foof, I couldn't help myself," Delia said. "I saw her leave with that dog—the kind I always wanted—and I just thought, humph. It's not fair."

Brianne stared at her grandmother. "Gram, what on earth are you talking about?"

Delia sighed. "Follow me," she said, turning and heading down the hall.

Brianne glanced at him, and they both followed her grandmother into what appeared to be her bedroom. She went to the closet, reached into a big black bag and pulled out a plastic-sheathed white lace dress with a ruffled hem.

Sometimes Ford's job did itself.

"What is that?" Brianne asked.

"It's Cole Harmon's fiancée's wedding dress," Delia said. "I snuck into her house once she left with her dog and I took it."

Brianne gasped. "What on earth for?"

"I thought the two of you were getting serious," Delia said. "Then he just tosses you aside and proposes to someone else? Who does he think he is?"

"Gram, you stole someone's property? A *wedding gown*?"

"I'm not proud of it, but yes. Sorry, Detective," she said. She held out her wrists again. "You can read me my rights now. I know them from watching decades of *Law and Order*. My favorite program."

Brianne dropped her head in her hands, then looked at Ford. "Are you going to arrest my eighty-four-year-old grandmother?"

"Tell you what," Ford said. "Give me the stolen property and a little time, and we'll take it from there."

"My grandmother is very sorry," Brianne said. "And I'm very embarrassed. Please let Cole's fiancée know how sorry we are." She handed him the dress.

"I'll be in touch," he said, heading for the door.

"Aren't you going to tell me not to leave town?" Delia asked.

He almost smiled. "Don't leave town."

Her eyes widened and she nodded.

"We'll be right here when you're ready to talk

about next steps," Brianne said, shooting her grandmother a chastising glance.

Once he was back in his vehicle, the dress folded in its plastic wrap on the seat beside him, he called Trudy Dunbar and said he had news. She told him to come right over and that she was now staying at Cole's house, soon to be their house.

When he exited his car at Cole's, the garment over his arm, Trudy came rushing out and called, "The detective has the dress!"

Danica, who was holding a crying baby, emerged from the house. She was accompanied by another woman, who looked a lot like her. As always, his heart skipped at the sight of Danica. She was dressed for work in a pale pink suit jacket and miniskirt, lots of jewelry, four-inch shiny heels and glossy lips. Her long blond hair was in a low, wavy ponytail over one shoulder.

"You found it!" Trudy exclaimed as Ford handed it to her. Trudy held out the dress to examine it. "Not a mark on it."

"Wow, that's great," Danica said, stepping down off the porch and bouncing the baby in her arms. "There, there," she said to the tiny girl. "Aunt Danica's got you. Everything's okay."

The baby cried harder, reaching out her hands for the other woman.

Danica sighed and handed over the baby. "Detective Ford Dawson, this is my sister, Candace, and her daughter, Brandy."

Ford nodded at Candace. "Nice to meet you. Adorable baby," he added, making a quick peekaboo at the little Brandy. The baby perked up, so Ford did it again.

Danica grimaced. "Does this child like everyone but me?" She smiled and shook her head.

"Brandy loves her aunt Danica," Candace said, smoothing the baby's curls. "I think when she sees you, she thinks you're me because we look so much alike, then realizes you're *not* and gets fussy."

"Huh," Danica said. "So it's not me. She just wants her mama."

Ford could tell Danica wanted to believe it but didn't.

Candace nodded, then turned to Ford. "Nice to meet you, too. I'm so relieved you found my aunt's dress. Where did you find it?"

"I think I'd better speak to Trudy privately about that," Ford said.

Danica and Candace eyed each other.

He gestured for Trudy to join him over by the tree. But before he could get a word out, a car came up the gravel drive to the house. Two women got out—Brianne and, more slowly, her grandmother.

The eighty-four-year old ambled up to Trudy. "I'm Delia Johnson, Brianne's grandmother. I'm very sorry I took your dress."

There were three sets of gasps.

"*You* stole my dress?" Trudy asked the elderly woman.

"You know I'm always watching everything in the neighborhood, and I saw when you came home yesterday with a dress bag from Bridal Dreams—just a couple weeks after Cole told my granddaughter it was over between them. I started stewing and when I saw you leave with that dog I sneaked right in the side door, looked for the dress and then sneaked back out with it folded under my arm. I hid it in my closet."

"I'm so sorry, Trudy," Brianne added. "And mortified. I have absolutely no hard feelings toward Cole or you." She sent her grandmother another chastising glance.

"Well, I do!" Delia said. "But it was wrong to take the dress and I deserve whatever happens. I fully expect to do some time in prison."

"Prison!" Trudy repeated. "Of course you're not going to prison. I'm willing to forget about this whole thing—if you promise on a stack of

Bibles never to break into my home again, Delia Johnson."

Delia's eyes widened. "Promise," she said. "You heard me swear it, Detective."

"I did, indeed," Ford said.

Danica stepped forward. "We have back the dress, so all's well that ends well." She turned to Ford. Thank you for everything."

"Yes, thank you, Detective," Trudy added.

There was a flurry of "I'm sorry" and "good-bye," and then Brianne and her dress-stealing grandmother were gone.

"Never saw that coming," Danica said. "Life never stops being one big surprise."

"Speaking of surprises," Candace said, "guess who I saw in the grocery store a little while ago when I went to get diapers? A guy I dated a few times in middle school. He asked me out for to-morrow night, and I was so caught off guard I said yes."

"Ooh, interested?" Trudy asked.

Candace shrugged. "I don't know. I'd really rather be matched the way Danica is doing it—based on what I'm looking for and all that. I'm done with making mistakes."

Ford noticed Danica's gaze slide over to him. Was that what he was? A mistake?

"Oh," Candace said, brightening. "He's a cowboy at your family's ranch," she added, turning to Ford. "Know him? Jasper Fields?"

Ford nodded. "Jasper's a great guy. Dependable, always offers to help out even when it's quitting time."

"That's some reference," Danica said.

Candace brightened. "Sure is. I'm kind of excited about the date now." She bit her lip, then looked from her aunt to her sister. "I'll need a sitter, though. I hate asking so last-minute. By any chance, are either of you available?"

Ford caught Danica's face slightly pale, saw the way she took a slight step back. Didn't take a detective to see that she was uncomfortable with the idea of babysitting her niece. Maybe because of how the infant had been bawling in her arms earlier?"

"I would, honey," Trudy said, "but I've got a big night tomorrow. I'm actually meeting Cole's whole family for the first time. His parents are throwing a big dinner party for us."

"That's so nice," Candace said.

"I'll babysit," Danica said. "I don't have much experience with babies, but I love my little niece, so that's something, right?"

"I'll help," Ford blurted out before he could

think about it. "I have too many tiny nieces and nephews to count, and have been on babysitting duty many times in the couple months since I moved back to Bear Ridge."

"My sister *and* an officer of the law babysitting my daughter," Candace said. She gave the baby's head a nuzzle. "You could not be in safer hands, darling."

Danica seemed about to say something and then clamped her lips shut. Ford had a feeling she didn't like the idea of babysitting with him, but she liked the idea of the *help*—and the help won out.

The plan was for him to arrive at Danica's at 7:15 p.m., a bit after the cowboy arrived to pick up Candace.

Well, this should be interesting.

Ford almost stopped to buy flowers for Danica, then remembered with an ice-cold poke in the gut that this wasn't a date. And that he really shouldn't have steamrolled his way into babysitting with her. But he wanted an explanation so that he could get past her, move on, fill out one of those matchmaking forms and see what happened. Besides, if Danica really hated the idea of him joining her tonight, she would have made some fast excuse and he would have backed off. She hadn't.

As he walked up the front steps to her house with the bag from Bear Ridge Toys—just a little something for her niece—he could hear a baby screaming bloody murder. He could see Danica through the big front window, pacing back and forth, rubbing the baby's back and looking exasperated. She was still in her work clothes, that sexy pink suit and high heels. He rang the bell and kept his eyes on her in the window. She glanced out and he waved, and the relief that crossed her features made him feel better about being here.

He heard the click of her heels on the floor, and then the door opened. She shifted the baby into her other arm and bounced her up and down.

"Look, sweet pea, it's Detective Dawson," Danica said with a mix of hope and exasperation.

Brandy kept sobbing. Sure was loud for a tiny person.

Ford smiled and reached into the little bag from Bear Ridge Toys. He pulled out the orange teether with rattling rings and twirly bits. He held it up to the baby girl. "This is for you, Brandy. Matches your pj's."

Brandy stopped crying and reached for the teether.

Danica bit her lip. "I tried three different toys and nothing worked."

"Probably the novelty of something new," he said.

"It was nice of you to bring her something," Danica said. She held the door open and he stepped in.

"Just get home from work?" he asked, wondering why she was still in her fancy little pink tweed suit and four-inch heels.

"Just fifteen minutes ago, right before the honorable cowboy arrived to pick up Candace," Danica said.

Brandy grabbed on to Danica's long swirly ponytail, which cascaded over one shoulder.

"Ooh, this little one's got some grip," she said, wincing and trying to get the baby's hand from her hair.

Brandy held on tight.

Ford distracted the baby and held out his arms. With what looked like clear relief, Danica handed her over. He held her against his chest, giving her back a rub. "Hey, there, cutie."

Brandy stared up at him with enormous blue eyes just like her mother and aunt.

"I should really go put up my hair and change," Danica said. "A client called just as I was about to head home and was dying to see a particular house, so I showed it but got here just before Candace's date arrived. I didn't have a chance to change."

"I've got Brandy. Go ahead."

She looked at him and then dashed up the stairs as quickly as was possible in those shoes. Halfway there, she stopped and took them off, then continued.

He moved into the living room, which was elegant, like Danica. The couch and love seat were white. "You know what doesn't mix, Brandy?" he said to the little one in his arms. "Babies and white couches. Let's head into the kitchen."

Ah. The kitchen showed evidence that someone actually lived in this house. A slew of baby bottles were lined up by the sink. A coffeemaker with about a cup left in the carafe. A big bowl of apples and bananas. The round table by the window was almost completely covered by papers— forms of some kind—and a legal pad.

"Much more comfortable," came Danica's voice.

He turned around—and swallowed. Danica wore a tiny white V-necked T-shirt and close-fitting pink sweatpants with a drawstring tied in a bow. One pull… Her hair was in a loose bun. She looked incredibly sexy. He'd only ever seen her all dressed up to the nines…or naked.

Her gaze moved to the table. "Mayor Abbott bamboozled me into taking over the matchmaking since I've been in town forever and know just about everybody, even the newcomers, since most of them came into the realty to see about vacation rentals."

"And as a bonus you can save the best ones for yourself," he said without thinking.

She shook her head. "Oh, I'm done with dating. I should have figured I'd have a tough time."

He stared at her. "Tough time? Why?"

Her face flushed for a second as if she hadn't realized what she'd said. "Oh, um, you know, dating is hard."

Was she talking about them? In general? "Yes, it sure is."

Brandy put little fists to her eyes and rubbed, then let out a yawn.

"Looks like it's someone's bedtime," he said.

Danica stepped toward him, reaching out her arms. "I'll take her." Brandy screeched, and Danica held up her hands. "Maybe you'd better carry her up."

Ford gently rubbed the baby's back and followed Danica out of the kitchen.

"We made a nursery of sorts in the spare room," she said as they walked to the stairs. She turned to look at Brandy, whose eyes were drooping, her cheek against Ford's chest. "I wish I had the touch with her, but I definitely don't," she said, hurrying up the steps and into the first room on the left.

A bassinet was between the windows in the dimly lit room. Danica took the baby and laid her down on the pad on the dresser and changed her, Brandy yelling her head off the entire time. Then Danica picked her back up and paced the room, singing under her breath what sounded like "Hush Little Baby."

Brandy cried harder, and Danica looked like she herself might burst out sobbing any second.

"I can try to settle her down," he said. "I babysat my twin niece and nephew a couple nights ago and got Chance to stop screaming in two seconds by making funny faces at him."

She handed the baby over, and Ford sat down in the rocker by the window.

"How about a story?" he asked the baby. "Once upon a time there was a llama named Dolly. Dolly was really funny looking with teeth that stuck out in weird directions. But she was a favorite at the Dawson Family Guest Ranch back when I was a kid." Brandy's eyes were drooping again. He smiled up at Danica, and the smile she sent him back was so warm and tender that he felt his heart move in his chest. He gave his throat a low clear. "Well, one day Dolly fell in love with a mean brown goat with a white spot on his head. And guess what happened? The mean goat fell in love, too, and was sweet to everyone, most of all Dolly, from then on. And they both lived happily ever after."

"Is that a true story?" Danica whispered.

"Every word," he whispered back. "And look— success. I'll just lay her down in the bassinet and cross my fingers." He stood up. Brandy quirked her tiny lips, but her eyes remained closed. He walked over to the bassinet and put her in, her arm shooting up by her head, her pink-and-purple-covered chest rising and falling with each sleeping breath.

"I'm not going to tell my siblings about this," he whispered as they left the makeshift nursery. "They'd make me babysit every night."

She didn't laugh. The smile wasn't back. She just headed down the hall, eyes on the Persian runner, then paused at the top of the stairs. "No one would ever ask me to babysit unless they were desperate, like my sister. If you hadn't come to the rescue, Brandy would probably still be crying her eyes out. Like I said, I just don't have the touch. Never have. Even when I babysat some as a teenager, I was bad at it."

"Well, then, lucky for you I was here," he said,

not sure exactly what to say, and whether he should probe or keep it light. It made him realize how little he actually knew Danica, how little of herself she'd revealed during their night together.

"You said you wanted six kids. At least four." She turned away. "I'm not sure I want kids at all. Even one."

He stared at her, then reached for her hand, which she allowed him to hold. "Is that why you left on me?"

She nodded. "Everything in me froze up, Ford."

"Yeah, I know what that's like. Before I felt ready for marriage, whenever a woman I was seeing would bring up commitment or getting engaged, everything in me would freeze up, too."

She tilted her head. "So you understand. That's a relief. I'm sorry I didn't just say something at the time. The subject always makes me feel so inadequate. Like I don't want something I'm supposed to want."

"You're not supposed to want anything," he said. "How you feel is how you feel."

He could see her shoulders relax. She seemed to take that in, nodded and then headed into the kitchen. "Coffee?"

"I'd love a cup," he said.

She washed out the carafe and made a fresh

pot, then pointed at the papers all over the table. "Maybe we'll find you a match in here."

So that was it? No discussion?

Then again, what was there to discuss? He did want a big family. She wasn't sure she wanted even one child. The smart thing would be to walk away from each other, as she had. Because if they started a relationship, a few years down the road, when he was itching to see toddlers trying to climb on the tire swing hanging on the big oak in the front yard of his farmhouse, she would be shaking her head. She'd say, *You knew I was up-front.* He'd say, *That's true, but.* And there'd be a stalemate. Ford knew how stalemates usually went. Resentment. Anger. Slammed doors. Then barely a goodbye.

She poured two mugs of coffee and they sat at the table. "I woke up early this morning to see if I could make a few matches before work, and I have five successes." Her smile lit up her face. "My ability to date might be complicated, but I can bring others together, right?"

He was about to say that he was sure there were plenty of men in town who didn't want kids. He used to be one of them. Same with all his brothers, all four of whom were now doting dads. But the thought of her with someone else? Made his stomach twist. He mentally shook his head, knowing he was in for something here. Trouble.

"I haven't found a match for you yet," she said, sipping her coffee and picking up a form.

"Me?" He glanced at the paper in her hand. Wait a minute. Was that his photo in the upper right-hand corner?

She waved it. "Ford Dawson. Age 35. Never married. Dedicated detective on the Bear Ridge P.D."

He frowned. "I did *not* fill out a matchmaking request! Let me see that."

"That *is* you," she said, tapping the photo and handing him the form.

Ford scanned the page, which had been submitted online. He shook his head. "This has my sister, Daisy, all over it. 'What I'm looking for,'" he read. "'Just someone I connect with. She can be anything or anyone, but she likes dogs and wants or has children.'" He glanced at Danica. "Tell me you don't like dogs. That'll make it easier for me to put you out of my head."

Her almost-smile got him in the gut. "I love dogs."

"So there's just that one big, fundamental thing standing in our way," he said.

"It destroyed my marriage," she said. "There's

no point in starting something," she added on a whisper.

So why was he finding it impossible to think of her only as a friend?

"I'll find someone for you and you can find someone for me," she said with definitely too cheery a smile. Too forced. She was trying to get him out of her head.

What he should do was leave. The baby was asleep. All was well on that front. He should walk out the door and let Danica Dunbar get on with her life, find someone compatible.

"I'll need a lot more caffeine for that," he said, instead of getting up and running for the hills.

This time her smile was genuine and went straight to his heart.

Chapter Four

Danica slowly picked up a profile she'd noted earlier would be a match for Ford. She glanced at him, sitting beside her at the kitchen table, wondering if he had any idea how hard this was for her. There had been so much between them the night they'd shared, but their relationship couldn't go anywhere and that had to be that. *Let it go. Let him go, as you have for the past two months.*

"'Lily Mallard, thirty-four, single, social justice warrior lawyer now ready to meet her match and start a family,'" Danica read, biting her lip as she stared at the three photos Lily had attached to her form. In one, she wore a power suit and killer heels on the steps of city hall in Brewer, and was kneeling beside an adorable cinnamon-colored shepherd mix, matching red-and-white bandannas around both their necks; another featured Lily in jogging clothes. And the third showed her in a pretty summer dress with the Bear Ridge River behind her. Dammit. She sounded kind of perfect for Ford.

She held up the photos, and Ford barely glanced at them.

"No can do," he said. "Conflict of interest. I issued her a speeding ticket three weeks ago coming off the service road."

Danica tried to hide her relief and smile. But this was wrong. She had to find the man someone to fall for so that they could move on. Except she was in a holding pattern, and a man who'd moved on from her would not be here right now helping her babysit.

She held up another profile of an attractive blond with an amazing body. "'Lexie Parks. Thirty-three. Divorced. Newcomer to town from Cheyenne. Loves hiking, Mexican food and watching Wyoming Wildcats games.'"

"Nope," he said. "A couple weeks ago she called in a complaint about her neighbor's dog, fourteen years old with cancer, blocking the sidewalk when the dog clearly needed to rest."

Danica grimaced. "Ugh. I don't think she'll match with anyone."

"Oh, trust me. She will. You don't want to know an eighth of what I've seen from humanity."

She regarded him for a moment. "I'm glad you're here in Bear Ridge. I know there's crime everywhere, even tiny towns like ours, but it's got to be a little easier on you here, right?"

"It is. Yesterday, a wedding dress stolen by an eighty-four-year-old perp and a spurned lover who wouldn't stop serenading a woman outside her house were the only two reported crimes."

Danica grinned. "Mayor Abbott said there was a lid for every pot. Do you agree?"

"Yup. Just have to find each other."

"Well, that's where we come in for each other. Matchmaking buddies!" she added, aware she'd put on her fake cheery smile.

"This is awkward as hell, Danica."

She put down the next profile she'd set aside as a possible match. "Yeah, but we're friends now. And I like that. I'd rather have you as a friend than the big fat nothing we had for the past couple of months."

He held her gaze for a moment, then finally said, "Oh hell, me, too. So let's see if I can find someone for you in here." He picked up a stack of male profiles and scanned a few. "No," he said, putting the top one down. "Definitely not. Nope. Yeah, right." He shook his head. "I give that last guy credit for taking a shirtless selfie with that beer belly. He is who he is. But he's not right for you."

"Why not? Or that guy. Or that one. Or that one?" She gripped her coffee cup to have something to do with the hands that itched to touch Ford. His shoulder. His back. All that thick, silky dark hair. She glanced down, face flushed, as memories of their night together came over her. Ford unzipping the back of her dress. His gasp at the sight of her in just her bra and underwear. Danica liked sexy underthings and always wore lacy, satiny, pretty bras and matching undies. Her ex had stopped responding to her physically years ago, his interest having waned, and it had taken a terrible toll, doing a number on her self-esteem. Ford's reaction had made her so damned happy.

"One's been divorced four times," he said. "Another gets arrested at least twice a month for drunk and disorderly. And that one," he added, pointing, "says any woman he dates would have to deal with weekly dinners with his mother, who he describes as hell on wheels."

Danica smiled and picked up one of the forms.

"And what's wrong with this one? 'Looking for a kind, funny, interesting woman who's been through a thing or two and is still standing, like me. She should probably love movies, sharing popcorn, and the idea of growing old together on our porch with three dogs.'"

Ford tried to hold back his scowl. "He doesn't say anything about kids either way. So you'd have to meet, and the subject would have to come up. I mean, why put in the investment at all?"

The man did *not* want her to date. The goose bumps that traveled up her spine at the thrill of that were soon replaced by little chills. They could like each other, be attracted to each other all they wanted. It wasn't going to make them want the same things.

A cry came from upstairs.

They both shot up, and it was clear he also needed the break from how personal things were getting.

"Hope your sister's date is going well," he said as they went upstairs.

"You should have seen them when he picked her up. Both of them all smiles, stealing peeks at each other." She bit her lip. "I'm just so glad Candace is here. Our family has never been close, not even when Candace and I were young, and now she's staying with me and I'm babysitting my niece. I can't tell you how happy that makes me."

The warmth in his blue eyes almost undid her. She was already exposing too much of herself. "I'm glad for you. Your sister and niece are here. Your aunt is here. I know how important it is to be close to family. For a long time, I lived hours away because I felt close to my siblings no matter what," he said. "But after a while, I needed them in my daily life."

She held his gaze for a moment on the top step and nodded. He seemed about to say something, but another shrill cry came from the nursery and they headed in. Danica rushed over to the crib and leaned in to pick up the baby. Brandy started screeching like crazy, and Danica took a step back.

"You've got this," he said. "If you want to be close to Brandy, you've got to develop a relationship with her. So go show her who Aunt Danica is and what she's made of."

"Not very strong stuff," she said with a frown. "I always think I'm strong and independent, and then something will happen that makes me feel like porcelain."

"Yup, ditto."

His kindness rallied her, and she reached into the crib and picked up her screeching little niece.

Brandy looked at her and scrunched up her face. Danica held her straight against her chest, letting her legs dangle some in case she had a gas bubble. In anticipation of babysitting, she'd spent a good hour this morning with her phone, researching all kinds of baby-related facts. She rubbed Brandy's back, and the baby quieted down and yawned.

Danica looked at Ford and smiled, something tiny fluttering in her chest and stomach. "Better now, sweet pea?" she whispered to the baby, whose eyes were drooping. She gently rocked Brandy, humming an old lullaby she'd never forgotten, and now Brandy seemed to be asleep. Danica set her down in the crib, and she and Ford tiptoed out.

"That felt good," she said. "Maybe I can learn how to be an auntie yet. Thanks, Ford. I owe you."

"I'll call it even for a slice of whatever that was on the counter. Cheesecake?"

"Raspberry cheesecake. I could use another cup of coffee, too."

For the next fifteen minutes they had their treat and coffee, Ford telling her funny stories about babysitting his baby nieces and nephews, who the shriekers and spitter-uppers and unfussy ones were. They talked too easily. Laughed too hard. And this felt too right.

But then a car turned in the driveway, and a

door slammed and heels could be heard clicking on the walk. Ford brought their plates to the sink, and before they could turn around Candace was stalking into the kitchen, her hands balled into fists at her sides as she paced, steam coming out of her ears.

"Uh-oh," Ford said.

"You okay?" Danica asked her sister.

"How is possible for someone to be that arrogant?" Candace asked. "That much of a know-it-all? How dare he!"

The problem with not knowing her own sister well was that Danica wasn't sure how badly the night had gone. Had the cowboy from Dawson's Family Guest Ranch been a jerk? Or had they just not been a match?

"I'm surprised to hear this," Ford said.

"He's impossible!" Candace said, throwing up her hands. "We didn't agree on a single thing all night. We're total opposites. The date ended before the poor waiter could even ask if we wanted dessert. No, thank you!"

"But he was a gentleman…" Danica prodded.

"Well, yes. And do you believe he had the nerve to walk me to the door and not even ask if he could kiss me good-night? I mean, if he had, I would have said no, but still!" Candace stalked up the stairs, then turned. "I'm sorry I'm full of complaints. Thank you both for babysitting. Just a peek at Brandy will make me feel better about my awful night." She hurried the rest of the way up the stairs.

Danica looked at Ford. "Guess I'd better find someone new for my sister to get her spirits up."

Ford shook his head. "I'd hold off. Sounds like she and Jasper are about to fall madly in love."

Had he lost his mind? "What? Did you hear a word she said?"

"Yup. Remember when we met at your office for the first time and I argued with you about everything? We couldn't discuss square footage without it getting heated."

She'd forgotten that she hadn't liked him at all at first, that he'd been an arrogant know-it-all hiding under a polite demeanor. Because when she did start liking him, the feeling had gone from zero to sixty in a hot second. "I said black, you said white. You said up, I said down. I guess at the housewarming party, I started looking at you in a different way. Suddenly, you were in the midst of your big family, and I saw how close you all were and how doting you were to your little nieces and nephews. You won my heart that day, Ford Dawson."

Oh, God. Why had she said that? Yes, he'd won her heart, and she'd had to take it back.

"Ditto," he whispered, staring at her, and if this was any other guy, there'd be an amazing kiss. But it was Ford and so he took his leather jacket and Stetson off the coatrack.

"Well, let me know if I'm right about your sister and Jasper."

"I will," she said. "And thanks again for helping me out tonight."

"Anytime, Danica." He shrugged his incredible arms and shoulders into the jacket, put on the cowboy hat, tipped it at her and left.

She let out a breath and closed her eyes.

"Ooh, I might have a bad night, but you definitely had a good one," Candace said, coming down the stairs, eyebrows raised.

"Brandy still asleep?" Danica asked.

Candace nodded. "I stood by her crib watching her sleep, and everything went right with the world again. So, what's the deal with you and the hot detective?"

Danica felt tears sting her eyes.

"Oh, man, sorry," Candace said, taking her hand. "How about we have some ice cream? I need a few scoops of something decadent."

"We just had cheesecake, but hey, what's another five hundred calories?" Especially when this was her sister, someone Danica had wanted to be closer to for so long. She'd eat five bowls of ice cream if it meant the two of them sitting down and really talking.

Danica got out the Ben & Jerry's, and Candace brought two bowls to the table, shoving aside the matchmaking forms.

Candace stuck her tongue out at the forms. "Ugh, I'm done with romance."

"Yup, that's what I said after Ford." She scooped out their ice cream—Phish Food with its gooey marshmallow and chocolate wonders—and they dug in.

"So what happened?" Candace asked.

"He wants six kids. I'm not even sure I want one."

"Yeah, I felt the way you do until I was suddenly pregnant," Candace said. "The idea of a child, of my own family, seemed so alien. I mean, we didn't exactly have a close family."

Danica nodded. "The idea just seems so foreign. Like something I wouldn't really know how to do." She shook her head. "That's really sad."

"I was scared to death when I found out I was pregnant. But you know, you figure it out. I love Brandy. I actually love being her mother. And I'm good at it. I'm bad at just about everything else, it turns out."

"Oh, come on, Candace. You are not."

"I failed at even getting one-line commercials," her sister said, digging her spoon into her ice cream. "And I managed to fall for the biggest jerk in LA, who told me Brandy wasn't his and that I was a liar. I have to get motherhood right, Danica. I *have* to."

Danica put down her spoon, reached for her sister's hand and squeezed it. "You will. I know you will. And I'm here for you. So is Aunt Trudy."

Candace squeezed her hand back. "So should I stop dating or look for a good father for Brandy? Should I be working on myself? I don't know. I want to find a partner, someone to love, someone to love me. I want to feel *safe*. But I sure don't want to have more dates like tonight. I just want something easy. Something that feels *right*."

"I know what you mean. I think you just have to follow your instincts. And sleep on it. You'll feel better about everything in the morning."

Candace already seemed in better spirits from their talk and the ice cream. Danica felt her heart give another little leap of happiness. Here the Dunbar sisters were, sitting together, opening up, really talking. That they could grow close meant so much to Danica.

Candace finished the last of her ice cream. "This is just too good," she said, licking her lips.

"Amazingly good," Danica agreed, finishing her own bowl.

"Maybe you and Ford will find a way to work it out," Candace said, getting up to wash out the bowls and spoons.

Danica glanced at the stack of matchmaking forms. She thought about Ford's—filled out by his sister: *Just someone I connect with. She can be anything or anyone, but she likes dogs and wants or has children…*

Now she was going to lie in bed, tossing and turning because she'd be unable to stop thinking about him. When she had to. Maybe she would try to find someone for herself in the fresh stack coming her way tomorrow. But who was going to outdo Ford Dawson?

The next morning, Ford got up way too early—Danica Dunbar on the brain. He had two cups of coffee. He ran four miles. He oiled a creaky hinge on a door and did two loads of laundry. Nothing got Danica off his mind. He couldn't stop thinking about how she'd opened up to him, how vulnerably honest she'd been. Then his mind traveled back to February, in his bed. And to last night, sharing cheesecake, funny stories.

That he had strong feelings for her wasn't in doubt. But he did want a big family, just like the one he'd grown up in. He wanted children catapulting themselves on him to wake him up on Sunday mornings, when he'd make sixty pancakes and a hundred strips of bacon. If only he'd met Danica a year ago, when he'd still been in his "not ready" stage, which had lasted years. Not ready to commit to anyone, to anything, other than his work. But he wasn't about to think that if he, of all people, could change his mind about wanting a family, anyone could. He had no right to *want* Danica to change her mind or imagine she would; how she felt was valid and that had to be respected.

So she was right. They weren't a match, and he had to start thinking of her as a friend.

A *friend* might stop by her house this morning with coffee and muffins from the great Bear Ridge Bakery, but there had already been blurred lines last night. He'd almost reached for her, yearning to have her in his arms, against him, to kiss her, touch her. But he hadn't, of course. Thankfully, her sister had come home just when he'd been bursting with insane levels of desire for her, so he'd left.

And still couldn't shake her from his thoughts.

It was just before eight, and he had two hours before he had to be at the PD, so he texted his siblings to see if anyone wanted to meet him by the main barn at the Dawson ranch, where they all lived, to help him look for the bane of his existence: the diary. The diary he was beginning to think he'd never find. And maybe it was better that way.

By eight thirty, Ford and his middle brothers, as he'd always thought of Axel, Zeke and Rex, from his father's second marriage, were down by the river on the ranch, about a half mile down from the main barn. Ford had a shovel, Axel and Zeke had metal detectors, and Rex had a pitchfork. Once a week or so, Ford came out here with the hand-drawn—definitely *drunkenly* drawn—map his father had bequeathed him when he'd died a year and a half ago. Bo Dawson hadn't had much to his name, but he'd left all six of his children either letters or something personal tucked into an envelope. His sister, Daisy, had finally gotten her mother's wedding rings that she'd been asking for since she was eleven; they were all surprised their father hadn't sold them long ago for booze or a horse race. Ford's envelope had contained the map, scrawled in marker.

Apparently, when Ford was very young, his father had found his wife's diary, didn't like what he'd read, stuck it in a metal fishing tackle box and buried it somewhere on the property. Ford had overheard his mother talking to a friend about that, and every day he'd go outside at five years old, trying to find it to make his mother less upset. He never found it. Neither had his mother, and Ford remembered her looking with her own metal detector and shovels, poking into the earth. When he'd inherited the map, Ford had gone to visit that friend of his mother's to ask for more information, but the woman had been cagey, telling him only that Ellen Dawson hadn't ever found it, got madder and madder, had finally had it, and packed up and left her husband, taking Ford with her and re-settling across town.

Bo had remarried, had three more kids, then divorced again and married his third wife. They had two more kids—Noah and Daisy, both of whom would be helping right now, but Noah, the manager of the Dawson Family Guest Ranch, was at a cattle auction and Daisy, the ranch's guest relations manager, had a guest emergency.

For a long time, Ford hadn't wanted to find the diary. God knew what it said. Bo's drunken exploits, including with other women? His mother's anguish? Something had driven Bo to get rid of the diary. Was it documentation of something he'd done, or that Ellen Dawson had done? The wondering had made Ford tired. It wasn't his business. But it was *unfinished* business. And unfinished business had a way of poking into raw spots until it was dealt with.

So whenever he visited his siblings for a birthday or holiday, he'd come out here with the map and a pitchfork and stab at the ground, trying to hit the metal box that the diary was buried in. Since he'd moved back to Bear Ridge, he'd been trying to find it in earnest. Something told him he'd make peace with his father, with his parents' marriage, with how little he really knew, if he read it. He'd lost his mother when he was twenty-one and in the police academy, but she'd never liked talking about her first husband when Ford had been growing up.

His siblings had found that peace through dealing with what Bo had left them in their bequest envelopes. Ford was 99 percent sure it was the final step on this strange transformation of his. From city cop to small-town detective. From saying buffalos would fly across Wyoming before he'd ever move back to Bear Ridge. Now he was living here, serving the community. To being so confirmed a bachelor that he'd never committed to any woman, even when he was aware he did have feelings, to finally giving in to his heart. He'd gotten slammed for it; the woman he'd been involved with back in Casper had left him for someone else who was more this and more that; apparently, she felt she'd waited too long for him to come around, and by then it was anticlimactic instead of the start of something beautiful.

He'd spent a fitful few months stalking around Casper until he realized it was time to go home. To face who he was, who he'd been and how those two meshed. Time to find the damned diary and settle things in his chest with his father. Here he was. And his siblings, who he could always count on, even at eight thirty on a cold April morning, were right here with him. The three who could be, anyway.

"Dad's drawing might be that cluster of trees," Zeke said, gesturing at the maples. He peered over at the map, under Ford's foot at the moment so they could see it without it blowing away in the light wind. "I mean, the drawing looks nothing like those trees, but the cluster does. And remember how Gram and Gramps used to tap these trees for syrup? Maybe Dad was drawn here for that reason."

Huh. Bo Dawson had been surprisingly sentimental for someone whose actions said he didn't give a damn about anything, so that was possible. And Ford was pretty sure he'd dug into just about every inch of ground leading away from the barns. But he hadn't been down here. Axel and Zeke started going over the area with their metal detectors while Ford and Rex stabbed at the grass, still hard patches this early in the spring, with their tools.

Ford watched them for a moment, sometimes unable to believe they were really all here. All three of his middle siblings had fallen for single mothers of babies when all three had sworn off dating single mothers for pretty much the same reason Ford had: not ready, would never be ready, for family life, for commitment. Love had conked his younger brothers over the head one after another. Zeke, the businessman of the family, who'd opened a consultancy on Main Street and found love with his administrative assistant, who'd loved him since middle school. Zeke had actually had a long-time crush on Danica from high school, but when Zeke had moved back to town a couple months ago, he quickly discovered that he only had eyes for Danica's best friend, Molly Orton. Now they were engaged, and Zeke doted on her year-old daughter.

Then there was Axel, the director of safety for the ranch and a wilderness guide for guests. A former search and rescue worker and lone wolf, Axel had found a missing toddler on a mountain, reunited mother and son, and found himself unexpectedly joining a family.

Rex, who'd left the US Marshals and was now a cop at the Bear Ridge PD with Ford, had found an old bottle in the Bear Ridge River with an old letter to Santa inside from a foster child with a Christmas wish: to be adopted. He'd felt compelled to find Maisey Clark and make sure her wish had come true. He ended up marrying the single mom of a baby girl.

And rebuilding the ranch had brought his brother Noah together with Sara, his first love, and her twin babies. Sister Daisy, who'd been pregnant and alone when she'd come home, had fallen for a man—very reluctantly at first—who'd come to claim the Dawson Family Guest Ranch as belonging to his family, but had surprised everyone by falling madly in love with Daisy.

And here was Ford, the oldest at thirty-five. Unable to let go of a woman he couldn't have. He'd just have to. Ford was nothing if not disciplined.

"So have you been matched with anyone yet?" Rex asked with a grin, his blue eyes—the same blue eyes all the Dawson siblings had—lighting up. He shot a glance at their brothers, whose grins gave them away.

"So it was you guys who filled out that form for me," he said. "I was about to go yell at Daisy for that."

"Nope, it was us," Zeke said. "We've noticed you haven't been going out much the past couple months, so we took matters into our own hands now that there are a ton of women in town. So how'd we do? Go on any dates yet?"

"Nope," he said, stabbing at the ground. "I'm on hiatus."

"Because of Danica?" Rex asked. "We were all at your housewarming party. We all saw you two lip-locked—more than once."

Slam. He suddenly remembered giving Danica a tour of the house well into the party, and suddenly they were kissing in a dark corner, and he couldn't wait for the party to end and everyone to leave so they could explore each other more. Which they had.

"Not meant to be," Ford said. And clearly glumly, because his brothers all stopped metal detecting and poking at the ground and stared at him.

"Gotcha," Zeke said, clapping him on the back.

"Well, when you want to start dating again, just

let us know and we'll exaggerate on your match-making form so you sound like a catch," Rex said with a grin.

"You can count on us," Axel added, pretend socking Ford with a one-two punch in the stomach.

Ford rolled his eyes, but he was touched. His brothers had his back. Noah and Daisy did, too. He was lucky and he knew it.

They spent the next hour trying to find the diary but came up empty. No surprise there. And then they'd all had to get going: Zeke, mind like a ledger, reminding them all that the twins' birth-day party was this weekend. Little Annabel and Chance—Noah and Sara's children—were turn-ing a year old.

Ford was heading through the gates of the ranch when he noticed Jasper Fields, the ranch hand who'd gone out with Candace last night, about to pass him in his pickup on his way in to work. Jas-per waved and slowed, and Ford stopped and rolled down his window.

"I'm not going to get fired for that fiasco of a date with your friend's sister, am I?" Jasper asked. Ford could see that the guy was serious. He truly looked worried.

"Of course not," Ford assured him. "Date disasters go hand in hand with dating. Sometimes a couple just doesn't mesh."

"That's the thing," Jasper said, running a hand through his tousled blond hair. "I thought we did. Candace Dunbar has to be the prettiest woman I've ever seen in my life. But then we started arguing about country versus city life and then whether babies should be picked up immediately when they cry in the middle of the night or not, and suddenly, she's telling me I don't know everything and asking for the check. I was hoping to take her dancing, but the night ended way too early."

"Know much about the sleeping habits of babies, do you?" Ford asked.

He shrugged. "I was just trying to act like I knew what I was talking about. I knew when I asked her out that she had a baby, so I went home and googled some facts. I was trying to get across that I was interested in what she was saying."

Ford smiled. The guy tried so hard it had backfired. "Well, maybe you could ask for a do-over. See how it goes."

Jasper brightened. "A do-over. Yeah… I will. Hey, thanks, Ford."

As he watched Jasper's truck head through the gates and up the road that would lead to the main barn, he chuckled. He'd called that one. There would definitely be a second date, a second chance.

And maybe he could help Danica babysit again. Of course there could be no second chance for them. But he sure liked the idea of spending time with her.

Chapter Five

Danica rarely used her vacation time, but she asked for the week off so that she and her sister and niece could spend time together and also help with Aunt Trudy's wedding preparations. Thanks to a cancellation, Trudy and Cole had managed to snag one of the small ballrooms in the lodge at the Dawson Family Guest Ranch lodge, a beautiful white building with a steeply pitched roof that overlooked Clover Mountain and had a spectacular view. The three of them were in the ballroom now and had been for the past hour, Trudy deciding on the color of the runner and guest chairs for the ceremony, the arrangement of the tables for the reception and, of course, the flowers. Danica had been drawn to the windows, imagining Ford, who'd grown up here, running up and down the halls of this level of the lodge with his sister and brothers as a young boy, climbing the mountain in the near distance.

On the drive over she'd wondered if she'd run into him, then realized of course she wouldn't. She'd been his Realtor, after all, and knew exactly where he lived—in a renovated farmhouse right in town. But he could be visiting his family, and if she happened to catch a glimpse of him she wouldn't mind one bit. Just being here on the property made her feel connected to him, a feeling she wasn't used to. But he'd shared some of his family history with her, the story of the ranch, how his grandparents had started the original guest ranch over fifty years ago, how his father had inherited it and quickly destroyed it, how the siblings had banded together to reclaim their legacy and rebuild.

Danica loved this room with its polished dark wood floor, warm white walls and the huge arched windows, three along the back wall. Somehow, the space managed to be both rustic and elegant at the same time. Neither Trudy nor Cole had big families, and they weren't expecting more than forty people.

"How many people were at your wedding?" Candace asked Danica. "Over two hundred? Maybe even three hundred?"

"Two eighty-four," Danica said, and she'd barely known half of them. Her ex-husband had a huge family and they'd run the show, including the guest list, particularly once they'd learned that Danica's mother didn't intend to help plan the wedding at all. Danica's former mother-in-law had been thrilled not to have to deal with the mother of the bride.

Danica had had misgivings about marrying Troy, but she'd been twenty-one, they'd been a couple since middle school, and he was a golden boy whose big family, very involved in Troy's life, drew her. She wanted to be a part of the family, in attendance at loud, huge family dinners. And in the early years, his mother and grandmother and aunts had welcomed her with open arms, their "Dani" that they'd known forever—until she was about twenty-five and a grandchild wasn't forthcoming. With each passing year, they got colder and colder, pushier and pushier, demanding she see a doctor to find out why she wasn't getting pregnant. She'd finally burst out with the fact that she was on birth control and wasn't sure she wanted a child. Her mother-in-law had stopped speaking to her. Troy had started his affair soon after or maybe even before. But he used it to excuse the affair.

She'd been disappointed by the Dunbars' lack of warmth and disinterest in family connection, family ties. Then she'd been dumped by in-laws for not being what they wanted. Somewhere along the way, her confusion over what she wanted got stronger and stronger, and keeping her distance from people became the new normal. She let out a sigh, hating all this muck. Right here, right now, was a new beginning with the women in this ballroom: Aunt Trudy, Candace, herself, and baby Brandy. Brandy would not grow up without a strong, supportive family.

"I think Trudy's wedding sounds absolutely perfect," Danica said. "Forty people, small and intimate, close friends and family. The people you love and care about with you on the happiest day of your life."

Her aunt beamed. Danica loved seeing Trudy, who'd been through the wringer, so happy. Trudy's phone pinged with a text and she pulled it from her purse. "Oh, what a surprise," she muttered, shaking her head. She dumped her phone back in her bag with quite a frown.

"What's wrong?" Danica asked.

"Guess who's sorry but unable to make it to the wedding and sends best wishes for a lovely event," Trudy said, looking from Danica to Candace.

Danica knew instantly the text was from her parents, and she felt the usual clench in her chest. Her parents weren't exactly cold, just standoffish and extreme introverts. And now they had the excuse of living hours away and "you know we don't travel well."

Candace's expression said she knew it, too. "I just don't get it. I mean, I do. I've been like them, too. For too long. But I see where that's gotten me. Feeling alone. *Being* alone."

"I guess they have each other and that's always been enough for them," Danica said.

"I'm a witch, but I'll tell you," Trudy said, "your mother steers that ship. My brother was more family oriented until he married your mother. No offense."

"None taken," the sisters said in unison, then both gave dry laughs.

"But it's been what, thirty-five years they've been together," Trudy said, "and they are who they are. I accepted it long ago. To the point that I let my husband steer our ship and keep me from reaching out to you two more. I was just so used to being basically estranged, and he wanted no part of family obligations." She let out a breath. "Awful."

Danica nodded. "Well, we're together now and it's a fresh start. Especially for this little beauty," she added, kneeling down in front of Brandy's stroller to gently cup the baby's chin.

"To fresh starts," Trudy said, holding out her hand.

Danica smiled and put her hand on Trudy's, and Candace put her hand on Danica's.

Then they bent down and put their hands under one of Brandy's tiny ones.

Just as the door opened, they heard a familiar voice. "Oh, sorry, I didn't realize this room was occupied."

Danica turned just as her best friend, Molly, was hurrying out, her long, wildly curly brown hair bouncing behind her. "Molly, wait! It's fine!"

Molly turned, her baby daughter, Lucy, in a carrier on her chest, and her mouth dropped open. "Danica? I didn't even register that was you."

Danica glanced down at herself. She usually didn't leave her house without being dressed to the nines, even on Saturday morning runs to the coffee shop—and that included full makeup, hair flat ironed and curling ironed to beachy wave perfection. Her skin care regimen alone took thirty minutes and had nine steps. But since she'd morphed into full-time Aunt Danica, she rolled out of bed, took a fast shower, twisted her hair into a bun so that tiny fists couldn't yank the long strands, and wore comfortable jeans and tops that didn't require dry-cleaning from baby-spit up. Right now, Danica was in a simple T-shirt dress with a jean jacket and ballet flats, something she'd normally wear to a baseball game. And had she even put on makeup this morning? She'd gotten up early with Brandy, and honestly, she couldn't remember if she'd bothered with even mascara. And Danica was usually a five-coat gal. This new her took so much less effort, and now she wondered if she'd been hiding behind all that gloss and veneer. She'd never looked at it that way before; she'd just taken herself for a girly girl who liked glamming it up.

"Guess who's visiting and hopefully moving to Bear Ridge permanently with this little darling," Danica said to Molly. "My sister, Candace. You guys remember each other, right? Molly's been my best friend since second grade."

"I definitely remember you, Molly," Candace said. "And wow, I don't even think I have any friends from school anymore. That's impressive."

"Danica and I are forever," Molly said, giving

Danica a quick hug, taking care not to squish the baby between them.

"And hello to you, my sweet goddaughter," Danica said, gently caressing Lucy's pretty brown hair. She adored the baby girl but all the baby-sitting and outings with Molly and Lucy hadn't sparked baby fever for Danica.

Molly turned to Danica's aunt. "Nice to see you again, Trudy, and congrats on your engagement. Omigosh, are you having the ceremony here?"

Trudy nodded. "I love this room."

"Me, too," Molly said. "I've been looking at lots of venues, but I keep coming back to this particular one. Just look at those windows and that view."

Molly was engaged to Zeke Dawson, Ford's brother, who owned a consulting business in town. He and Molly were now full partners, even though she'd started as his administrative assistant. They didn't have a wedding date yet but were working on it.

"That's what we all said when we walked in," Candace noted, nodding and looking around the lovely space.

"Aw, the babies like each other," Candace said, pointing.

They all turned to see Brandy and Lucy staring at each other with big grins, batting their little hands in the air. Candace and Molly exchanged numbers so they could arrange a playdate for the girls, talking a mile a minute about the babies' schedules and habits and milestones, and Danica could feel herself stepping back, shrinking, not part of any of this. She'd picked up a lot in just a couple days of having a baby in her house, but she was the aunt, not the mom, and as she'd watched her sister take care of Brandy, really saw what went into motherhood on so many levels, she'd found herself feeling kind of scared. But if Candace had taken to being a mother, couldn't Danica, too? They'd been raised in the same home, the same way.

She was so lost in her thoughts that she'd barely heard Molly saying goodbye, and then it was again just the four of them in the ballroom. Trudy had her list of everything she needed to take care of for the wedding as did Danica and Candace, so they headed out.

"Oh, God, there he is," Candace said, eyes narrowed on a tall, muscular blond man in jeans and a cowboy hat, a saddle in his arms near the barn. "Jasper from last night."

Jasper noticed them, lifting his hand in a wave, then jogged over to a nearby pasture and knelt down. He shot up with a bouquet of wildflowers in his hand and jogged over. "Morning, Candace. These are for you," he added, extending his hand.

Candace eyed the flowers without a smile but took them. "Thank you."

"This beautiful baby girl must be Brandy," he said, making peekaboo faces at her. "Aren't you the spitting image of your mother."

Candace tilted her head. "Well, we don't want to keep you from your work."

He glanced a bit bashfully at Danica and Trudy, who took a step back to give the guy some privacy. "I'm hoping you'll give us a second chance, Candace. I think last night, we just had so much to talk about, so much in common, that we just both really got truthful instead of holding back and being all polite with each other. I think that's a good thing. I'd like to get to know you better."

"As long as you admit right this second that I know more about babies than you because I'm the one who has a baby," Candace said.

The handsome cowboy grinned. "You absolutely do. I was trying to show I related and that I like babies."

Candace smiled. "Well, then, I'm looking forward to that second date."

He pumped his fist in the air. "Hope you're

free tonight. I wanted to get started on our second chance right away."

"I'm happy to babysit," Danica said. "And, hi, I'm Candace's sister, Danica. We didn't have the chance to meet last night. And this is our aunt Trudy."

They shook hands and a time was set, and the cowboy loped away with another fist pump.

"Aw," Trudy said. "I like him."

Danica smiled. "Me, too."

"Me three," Candace said, "but I'm gonna be cautious. I can't afford to make mistakes with someone I might bring into Brandy's life."

Danica stared at her sister, struck by what she'd said. The mother bear protectiveness. Their own mother hadn't been that way. Not that there had been divorce and boyfriends coming in and out of the home, but careless sitters—a teen down the street who ignored them completely, a woman who brought over her boyfriend and sent the girls outside and locked the door for an hour. *I've been afraid of motherhood because of what I grew up with,* she realized. *Not necessarily because of who I am, how I am.* Huh, she thought.

Tonight she'd try looking at Brandy in a different light, imagining herself as a mom and the type of mother she might be. Maybe her maternal instincts would rise up and baby fever would come calling. Of course she'd tried that countless times during her marriage, and the feeling that other women seemed to have so effortlessly never even pricked the skin. But she wasn't that same Danica anymore, in a terrible, lonely marriage, made to feel that there was something wrong with her, something deficient.

This is *my* second chance, she realized. At this new person I've become—*am* becoming.

The thought sent goose bumps up her spine—in a good way.

Ford and his brother Rex were returning to the police station after lunch at the diner when a woman, midthirties, marched up to them. She wore floral scrubs and a name pin that showed she worked at the nursing home. She didn't look happy, that was for sure.

"I'd like to file a complaint about a breach of expectation," she said.

Rex glanced at him, then at the furious woman. "What was this breach of expectation about, ma'am?"

"I really don't like being called 'ma'am' but that's neither here nor there right now," she muttered. "Two nights out, I went on a date with a man who told me he'd like to get together again and then never called or texted. Not five minutes ago, I saw him through the diner window sitting with a blonde and having pancakes. And you *know* they spent the night together if they're having breakfast at the diner! What are my rights in terms of lodging a complaint?"

Did he have time for this? Ford understood that dating was a killer, but the petty complaints were blowing up the BRPD lines, and he was constantly being asked questions like this. "I'm very sorry, but he didn't break a law," Ford said.

"I don't care about him," the woman said. "I'm talking about the *town*. Bear Ridge and the mayor and the town council are in breach of expectation! Obviously, they bit off more than they could chew with their matchmaking request forms, and they're just putting any old couples together based on age. I had absolutely nothing in common with that man!"

"But then why does it bother you that he didn't call?" Rex asked.

The woman scowled. "Because he said he would. I was raised to do what I say I will." She lifted her chin and folded her arms across her chest. "It was my first date since my divorce," she added. A moment later, everything she'd said seemed to weigh on her shoulders and they slumped in defeat.

That was dating for you. Hell.

Ford nodded. He felt for the woman. "It's unsettling when someone doesn't do what they say they will." But really, Ford was used to that. He'd grown up with a father who'd said whatever it took to get through the moment. *I'm running out to the store to get you kids something for dinner.* Then not returning until the middle of the night—and drunk. Promising to drink less while chugging a tall can of beer before the start of the school day. Reminders of his children's birthdays and then forgetting. Ford knew he could count on his siblings and his fellow officers. The rest of humankind? He didn't have any expectations *to* breach.

The tension in her face softened. "That's exactly it. I don't like it. Don't say you'll call when you don't intend to."

"I hear you," Ford said with a compassionate nod.

Rex also nodded. "Dating is rough."

"Not for the faint of heart," the woman said, brightening at her fortitude to be out there on the singles scene.

Ford leaned a bit closer. "I have an idea. Why don't you head over to the town hall or the coffee

shop and pick up another matchmaking form—
you can also find one online. Start from scratch
now that you've got experience under your belt.
You can include exactly what you're looking for
and *not* looking for. *Honorable* is a good trait."

She lifted her chin, much cheerier than she'd
been two minutes ago. "I'll do exactly that. Thank
you, officers. You've been very helpful." She
turned and left, headed right for the coffee shop
across the street.

Ford and Rex resumed walking, waiting for the
light to change at the corner of Main Street.

"I sure as hell wouldn't want to be out there,"
Rex said with a mock shiver.

Got that right. *Nothing* about love was for the
faint of heart.

"Yoo-hoo, officers!" trilled a voice.

Ford turned to see Mayor Pauline Abbott hurrying their way with a thick packet in her hands.

The mayor pushed her square silver glasses up
on her nose. "Ford," she began, "At least twenty
women have complained to me—and members of
the town council—that they've heard you're not
partaking in the matchmaking despite being single, and so I'm wondering if you might do our dear
community a big favor."

Ford raised an eyebrow. He supposed *those* complaints could be considered flattering, but it was also scary as all get-out. When the social media blast and articles in the local and county papers went viral about the town seeking single women for its lonesome bachelors, he'd had newcomers—from the very attractive to the pushiest of the pushy— sidle up to him, eye his left hand and then start flirting like mad. He'd had to explain he wasn't on the market, which got him blank stares, protests, lectures and even anger—*jeez, just say outright that I'm not your type instead of making excuses!* His sister, Daisy, had called it the Bo Dawson curse. Women had always been drawn to their tall, good-looking father with his Clint Eastwood blue eyes and thick, tousled dark hair. His sons were dead ringers for him.

Out of the corner of his eye he could see Rex smirking.

"Lots of breakups and disappointing dates the past week," Mayor Abbott continued, "and now I have sixty-two new matchmaking request forms, even more in-depth as to what they're looking for and not looking for. You know Danica Dunbar, right? She's our matchmaking angel, and I wonder if you might partner up with her to work on these. As a team, you'll speed right through them. Oh, and we should really set up another speed dating event, and between the two of you, you'll get it all good to go in no time."

This sounded like a full-time job. Ford already had one of those. "Anything else?" he asked in a politely sarcastic tone, but she didn't seem to catch it.

"Oh, this will keep you busy in your spare time, so I don't think so. Thank you so much, Detective. You already give so much to Bear Ridge, so we really appreciate this."

Ford held back his sigh of resignation. "Happy to help," he said, though he wasn't sure he was.

"Now, Officer Dawson," she said, turning to Rex. "I know you've got a toddler, and a baby on the way, so you have your hands full."

Rex smiled. "I sure do."

Ford sent a surreptitious scowl to his brother as Pauline handed Ford the stuffed packet and ran off after someone else. God only knew what she was about to make them do.

"You, a matchmaker?" Rex said, laughing as they resumed walking toward the police station. "Now I've heard everything."

"Right," Ford said, shaking his head. "How'd I get roped into this?"

"Hey, get married and get busy with kids, and

you'll be instantly exempt from a lot of torturous volunteerism."

He'd been willing to settle down, hadn't he? Ford had come home fully intending to find his wife, have those six kids, make all those pancakes and strips of bacon on Sunday mornings. And then the one woman he wanted was the one who didn't want to turn that fantasy in his head into reality.

No kids. *Could* he commit to that? If he were deeply in love? If Danica Dunbar was the only woman for him?

He mulled that over, not getting anywhere, half-listening to Rex talking about the first birthday presents he'd gotten Noah's twins, something about a chair in the shape of a tiger and a bear.

At the PD, Rex got pulled away by the rookie who was shadowing him for the rest of the day, and Ford went to his desk. He took out his phone and opened up his message app, tapping on Danica's lovely photo.

Mayor Abbott just got me to agree to be your matchmaking partner and to arrange a speed dating event, he texted. Apparently, some in town are throwing fits on their bad matches and want their new loves ASAP. Got some free time tonight?

Echoing in his head was to say no so they didn't get in any deeper. One of them had to be gatekeeper here, and despite his badge, it wasn't going to be him. He had to be near Danica, had to see her. Even if they could just be friends.

He froze for a second. Wasn't that getting close to the "only woman for him" category?

His phone pinged with a text. Danica.

I'm on babysitting duty tonight—you were right about Jasper and Candace!—if you don't mind helping out again.

He smiled. See you at seven?
Perfect, she texted back.
I'll grill, if you'd like, he typed without thinking.
Even more perfect, was her response.
Far from perfect, actually, he thought. But spending time with Danica was just what he needed right now.

Chapter Six

Turned out there was something unsettling about being in her backyard with a man grilling steaks and asparagus, a baby in her playpen on the patio making adorable gurgling sounds. All that was missing was a family dog, maybe a snoozing cat.

It was too much. And it was magic. All at the same time.

Danica's ex-husband had grilled all the time, but immediately afterward he'd settle down in his chaise, filled plate on a small table beside him, tablet turned to a baseball game, and they'd eat in silence—well, except for the announcer and the crowd cheering or her ex yelling at the screen when his team didn't do well. It had always been like that, and they'd been together for so long—class couple from seventh grade—that there had never been a honeymoon phase.

When Ford had arrived, she'd immediately noticed his very quick and appreciative perusal of her. He'd actually done a double take, and the goose bumps had broken out all over her body. Once again, Danica of the four-inch stilettos and sexy pastel-colored suits, long blond hair always coiffed to stylized perfection, had on no makeup, her hair was in a loose bun at her nape, and she wore a comfortable pair of skinny jeans and a long pale yellow cardigan with a white cami underneath. And slip-on sneakers that felt like heavenly slippers. Babysitting wear. Danica's new look.

Oh, and she'd had an eyeful of him, too. Dark jeans. Black leather jacket. Green Henley shirt, rolled up on his forearms. She couldn't look at him—ever—without remembering that first kiss against the wall in his house. The kiss that had lasted at least thirty seconds before they'd come up for air and only because they heard someone whisper, "Get a room." And then, of course, being alone with him once all the partygoers had left. How he'd held her gaze while he'd unzipped her dress. The sight of his bare chest had made her knees truly wobble.

Their attraction was palpable, that was just a fact, so when he'd immediately asked her to lead him to the grill, she'd understood why. Distraction had been necessary. He'd grilled and she'd made a salad, watching him from the window, and she'd loved every peek he'd sneaked at her. They ate outside, conversation nonstop but light, avoiding talk of them. It was such a gorgeous night that Ford had suggested they pack the stroller and head into town so he could buy presents for his twin niece and nephew, who were turning one this Saturday.

Now they were in Bear Ridge Toys on Main Street, standing barely an inch apart by a huge display of stuffed animals, Brandy in her stroller in front of them.

That felt even weirder—and more magical. Again at the same time.

Her phone pinged with a text. Aunt Trudy. Danica read the text, not sure how she felt about it.

"Everything okay?" For asked.

Danica shrugged. "Aunt Trudy and Cole decided to elope. Instead of getting married at the lodge on Saturday, they're flying to Las Vegas to a fancy hotel, having the ceremony at a quickie wedding chapel, and then staying there for a week's honeymoon."

"You sound disappointed," Ford said.

"Well, it would be nice to attend her wedding, help her with the finishing touches. Being a part of the wedding planning made me feel like we were really on our way to becoming close. But I get it. They couldn't shake the bad vibes with the dress being stolen, and Trudy's still getting looks from one of the women, so they just want to fly off where nothing can touch them."

"That's the kind of wedding I figured I'd have if I ever got married. Vegas. Just me and my bride."

That got her attention. "So you did think about marriage at some point? As a possibility for yourself?"

"I've had mostly short-term relationships, but a few of my exes talked about marriage, and when I tried to imagine myself getting married, I couldn't. Or at least not some big wedding. Vegas seemed special in itself, just the two of us."

"I guess that's how Trudy sees it." She sighed. "I just want to be closer to my family. Now I won't even be going to my aunt's wedding."

"Sounds like she's planning to come back to Bear Ridge and settle down with Cole in his house. You two could work on building bonds then. You just keep inviting her, reaching out, opening up, and she will, too."

Danica nodded, about to thank Ford for, once again, not only understanding what she was trying to say but being supportive and compassionate.

"What a beautiful family!" said an elderly woman holding the hand of a young boy. "The baby looks just like both of you!" She smiled and the group moved on.

"Who wants to tell her?" Ford quipped. "Although Brandy does look a lot like you. You and your sister could be twins. And I suppose I do have blue eyes, just like you and our baby here." The moment the words were out, he choked to the point that he had to use his fist against his chest.

"We do look like a family out shopping for toys for our baby daughter," she said.

"Make you want to run for the hills?" he asked.

She glanced down for a moment, then back at Ford. "You know, to make pleasant conversation, clients, prospective clients, house sellers always ask if I have kids, and when I say no, they look so surprised. Then there's that moment of 'oh, maybe I shouldn't have asked because she probably can't have kids.' I always read that on faces. Then there's a brief awkward silence before I quickly fill it. So, when that woman mistook us for a family, all

I felt was…normal, Ford. For just a moment, like everyone else." She turned toward a huge stuffed panda holding a shiny satin heart, realizing she'd exposed too much of herself, not unusual when she was with Ford Dawson. He had a way of making her talk. Had to be a detective trait.

He squeezed her hand. "I've always admired people who march to their own drum."

She liked that, but she wasn't so sure that applied to her. "I married my ex-husband knowing something wasn't quite right. I went along. But with a baby, bringing a new life into the world? That was a firm no, not ready, not sure."

"Interesting," he said. "So maybe it's not that you don't want a child, Danica. Maybe you just knew you didn't have the right husband. The right family setup. Maybe you just recognized that and refused to 'go along anymore.'"

"Maybe. I don't know."

"You don't have to be sure of anything except that I shouldn't buy these giant pandas, right?" he said, gesturing behind them at the display. "Noah and Sara live in the foreman's cabin on the ranch. Despite it being small, it has history for both of them, so they want to stay there even though they're running out of room as the twins get bigger."

"Yeah, no giant pandas," she said, wanting to reach up a hand to his handsome face. She was so touched by how he was able to talk to her about the child issue, how he seemed to support her without saying too much. She appreciated it.

And instead of keeping him safely in the friend zone, she was falling further and deeper for him every time they were together.

Instead of the giant pandas, Ford bought two colorful play tables with lots to squeeze, press and bat at. Ford was a sucker for personalization, so when the owner offered to stencil the twins' names on their tables, he said yes, and then he and Danica and Brandy went to the coffee shop to kill the half hour it would take. They made it back to the shop just before closing at eight o'clock. Most of Bear Ridge's Main Street stores extended their hours with the warmer weather and since daylight saving time was keeping dusk later and later.

Now they were at Danica's house, the yawning, eye-rubbing Brandy easily put to bed. Ford and Danica were on the sofa, the matchmaking forms on the coffee table.

Ford picked up the first one in his stack. "'Lonesome cowboy seeks his one and only,'" he read.

"Aw, that's sweet," Danica said.

"Do you think there's a real 'one and only' for everyone?" Ford asked, reaching for the tall iced mocha he'd brought back from the coffee shop.

"I don't know. I think some people find theirs, and they're really, really lucky. And others may have to kiss a few frogs or frogettes. You can think you found your person and then discover they're not that anymore. Things can change."

"Yeah," he said. "Exactly that."

"Did you ever think you'd found yours?" she asked.

"You'd think by my age the answer would be yes, but if she came along I didn't recognize her. I think that may be another issue for people. Wrong timing. The perfect person might be right there, but you can't see it for whatever reason."

Were *they* perfect for each other—with the exception of that one big fundamental issue? All Ford knew was that until she'd left in a hurry in the middle of the night, he'd felt Danica Dunbar dead center in his chest, and he'd never experienced that before. He'd always heard people say "you'll just know." He *knew* that night back in February.

He was aware he was staring at her, wanting to touch her so badly he squeezed his drink cup too hard, so he glanced down at the matchmaking profile. "Thomas Whittaker, forty-two. Divorced.

Twin seven-year-old boys. Senior accountant. 'I'm looking for a hilarious, life-of-the-party type with a big laugh because that's me. Sure my job sounds dry, but numbers can be funny, too. Except when it comes to the number one. It's the loneliest number, right? Oh yeah, must love attending all rodeo championships and enjoy really boisterous children who will drive you insane in ten minutes.'"

Danica laughed. "He sounds great. And I know just the woman for him! A Realtor in my office—Carrie. Biggest laugh in Bear Ridge and loves the rodeo. He described her to a T. And she's very open about the fact that she wants to meet a single dad because she can't have kids." She rummaged through her stack until she found Carrie's form, holding it up. She peered over at the photo of Thomas. "Hey, they even kind of look alike! I have a good feeling about this!"

"That one was easy," he said, using a paper clip to attach the two profiles together. According to Danica, the protocol to pair matches involved one of the matches getting in contact with the other. One of the first boxes to check off on the form was whether you wanted to be the caller or the called or either. "Callers" wanted to see the forms they matched with and decide if they wanted to call the match. "The Called" wanted to be called by their matches if they passed muster. Thomas had checked off "The Called" and Carrie had checked off "Caller" which gave her the leg up in deciding if she wanted to match with him or not. The Callers would then receive an email with the matched profiles attached. The system was wonky, in Ford's mind—what if both checked off the same box—but it seemed to be working.

They went through five more forms, making five matches, and found more than one for a few, which required scanning the profile and attaching it to the matched request.

Danica sipped her iced coffee and set it back down, picking up another profile. "Okay, now we have Jolie Parkwell, thirty, single, high school social studies teacher, grew up on a ranch, hoping to meet marriage-minded man of character and integrity who wants a big family. 'I have a thing for a man in uniform, whether serving his community or country…'" She glanced up at him. "Well, I guess we'll just clip this one to your form. She sounds just right for you. Or a coffee to start, anyway."

He shook his head. "No way. I told you—I didn't fill out that form. And it turns out my sister, who lives for matchmaking, didn't either. My brothers did."

"That's even sweeter," she said. "They want you to have what they have."

"Still. I'm not in the mix here."

"Form says you are and she does sound just right, Ford. No reason not to meet her."

Except I have a thing for someone else, so what's the point?

That was the point, actually. That he had to let go of his feelings for Danica.

"Fine, I'll meet her. Now let's find someone for you." The idea made him sick to his stomach, but he poked through the profiles. Staring back at him was an old rival from high school who'd beaten him out for captain of the lacrosse team even though he was a couple grades behind. Good-looking guy. Real Estate Developer. *Hoping to meet a lovely woman, inside and out, who's looking for commitment. I should add, I like kids, have a bunch of cute nieces and nephews, but I'm meant to be an uncle and not a dad.* Damn—it was almost too perfect. He stared daggers at the guy's photo as he handed her the profile. "And this one is for you."

She took the form and smiled. "I remember him! He was a very popular senior when I was a freshman." He watched her read the form, her smile fading when she got to the part about what he was looking for. She put his profile on the coffee table and picked up her coffee. "I don't know, Ford. I'm not so sure I should date someone who's sure he's an uncle and not a dad. I mean, what if I'm struck by baby fever next year?"

He gave a slow nod, not realizing she was more ambivalent about the subject than resolute. Maybe they didn't have cross each other off their lists, after all. "But doesn't that knock out every guy?"

"Yes," she said, biting her lip. "I've been thinking about this, and until I know what I want in that department, I should probably just concentrate on myself. No dating. At all."

Huh. Of course, she could decide her ambivalence had always been for good reason: because she didn't want children, end of story. Or not. But the bottom line was that she was *not* available.

"Well," he added, wishing she didn't smell so good, that she wasn't sitting so close, that he didn't want to kiss her so badly. "Let's try to get through ten more."

Over the next hour, they did, making lots of matches. There was a growing pile of "difficult to match" forms, though, and they were determined to find at least one match for each of those. One man was triggered by redheads and petite women, and would prefer potential in-laws who lived more than three hundred miles away from the area. A hard-to-match woman wanted a fellow devout Christian who looked like "that hot actor who plays Thor."

"Got him!" Danica said, holding up a profile in triumph. "I mean, he's not Chris Hemsworth, but he's a blond rancher with serious muscles."

An hour later, they'd found at least one match for twenty profiles, and Ford couldn't bear to look at another request. They moved on to planning the speed dating event, deciding on the Saturday night after next. Ford insisted on charging a twenty-five-dollar fee because a nominal charge meant those who paid would take the event seriously; twenty-five bucks would get them appetizers and refreshments at "get to know you even better" stations. That idea led to Danica suggesting they hold the event in one of the lodge ballrooms at the Dawson Family Guest Ranch to make the setting more exciting and festive. The town hall had two large meeting rooms, but nothing about those rooms was romantic. Sara, Noah's wife, responded to Danica's text about setting things up. She and Maisey, his brother Rex's wife, were going to town on the decor, nothing too cheesy, she promised. They watched some YouTube videos on speed dating events to get the gist on how to set up theirs.

Some elements clearly didn't work, which had them both cringing and laughing.

"I like the idea of card tables for two, set a few inches apart for privacy. We can assign every entrant a number to be ID'd by, and they'll also be given either the letter *A* or *B*. *A*'s will stay seated at the tables. *B*'s will move every two minutes."

Ford nodded. "Sounds good."

"So from what we watched, how about if we give each entrant an index card to jot down those people they wish to be matched with. Once the speed dating time ends, we'll call for mingling. Then we'll go through the cards and match those who selected each other, and write down the registration numbers of each entrant's choices. The chosen can see photos and descriptions and decide if they want to match with who selected them, then they'll leave their cards with us and we'll go through those and—"

"Or I could ask my rookie, who likes creating apps, if he could develop something simple to streamline all this. Entrants could download the app and make their choices right there at the moment, and then the app does all the work."

"I'm for that," she said. "And completely zonked."

"Romance is hard work, but we knew that," he said.

Their exhaustion came at the right time because a car pulled into the driveway. Candace. Danica popped up, anticipation on her face. Even Ford was curious how the date had gone.

They waited. And waited. And waited. Finally Danica walked over to the window overlooking the yard and pulled aside the curtain.

"They're kissing," she said with a smile. "Now they're talking. Now they're kissing again." She dropped the curtain and darted back to the sofa. "He's walking her to the door."

They waited. And waited. Ford figured there was one hell of a good-night kiss happening on the porch.

Five minutes later, Candace walked in, a moony expression on her face. "Omigosh," she said. "I'm so glad I gave Jasper a second chance. He's wonderful in every way. And guess who's taking me and Brandy to the zoo tomorrow?"

Ford smiled. Tomorrow was Saturday and supposed to be a gorgeous spring day, low sixties and sunny. He'd be at his niece and nephew's birthday party at the ranch, which was going to be held outside behind the main house, where his sister Daisy lived with her husband and son.

"Thanks for babysitting, Danica *and* Ford," she added with a sly smile and a glance at her sister. "I'll just go get changed," she said to Danica. "Back soon."

"We got a lot accomplished," Danica said, collecting the matched forms. "I'll scan in the profiles that were on paper and email all the 'Callers' in the morning."

He didn't want to leave. "Thanks for helping me pick out the birthday presents for my niece and nephew."

"Anytime," she said.

They headed to the door, Ford walking as slowly as possible. Dammit.

"Well," he said.

"Well," she whispered back.

And what was supposed to be a friendly, quick peck on the cheek turned into something else because she clearly hadn't been expecting it and turned slightly at just the moment his lips made contact with hers. He felt that kiss everywhere, memories of their night together hitting him left and right. Danica kissing every inch of his body.

She stepped back, face flushed, eyes smoldering.

"I was aiming for a chaste peck on the cheek. Sorry about that," he said.

"Oh, trust me, I liked it."

"Yeah, me, too," he said, holding her gaze.

Footsteps on the stairs had them turning. Candace was coming down.

"We should probably get together tomorrow night," he said, "to get through the rest of the matches."

"Your house or mine?" she asked.

"How about mine? Seven?"

"Sounds good," she said.

He peered around her. "Bye, Candace. Glad tonight went better than last time."

"Me, too!" Candace said, her eyes lit up.

He finally opened the door and walked outside, and when he turned for a last time, he knew he was in big trouble here. Danica Dunbar had his heart.

Chapter Seven

On Saturday morning, Danica and her sister sat outside on the back patio, sipping their coffee and eating bagels with veggie cream cheese. Every now and then, Danica would stare at Candace, unable to believe she was really here, the older sister she'd longed to be closer to her entire life. Last night they'd been about to talk about their love lives, or lack thereof for Danica, when Jasper had called. Candace had disappeared into the guest room with her phone, and by the time Danica had heard Candace's door open almost two hours later, she had been practically asleep in bed.

Hey, she got it. Falling in love was magical.

Danica should know. She was going through it herself.

About an hour ago, they'd stopped at Cole's house to see Aunt Trudy and surprise her with her wedding gifts. They were covering the newlyweds' hotel room in Vegas and had gone a little overboard in a boutique in Prairie City, buying Trudy some sexy lingerie. Their aunt had been thrilled, and cried and hugged them both, and Danica had been left with a good feeling about the future of their family.

Once she and Candace had settled down with their breakfast outside, Brandy in a playpen with her favorite toys, Candace had told her all about her night with Jasper. He'd planned a mega date—a fancy dinner in Prairie City, followed by dancing at a country and western club because Candace loved country music. After, they'd parked at Harmony Overlook with a view of the mountains and stars and had talked, so easily, about everything for over an hour before they'd kissed, and then they'd kissed for hours. Jasper was in the process of buying a small but prosperous cattle ranch from a rancher ready to retire, and Candace liked how sturdy he seemed on all levels. Apparently, Candace had a new dream of her own poking at her, to open up a makeover shop in town, transforming women. With all the newcomers and focus on matchmaking and dating, Candace thought she'd have a steady stream of customers. Apparently, Jasper had been so positive and supportive that all the walls Candace had up came crashing down.

While she'd been waiting for the coffee to brew and the bagels to toast, Danica had demonstrated her real estate chops and called storefronts that were either empty or about to be, negotiated a rent that Candace could afford based on the last of her savings, and now Candace had appointments to check out the spaces tomorrow. Her sister would be putting down roots in Bear Ridge, and nothing made Danica happier.

"Okay, so tell me what's going on between you and Ford," Candace said, taking a bite of her bagel. "And something clearly is."

Danica looked at Candace, then took a sip of her coffee. "Something is. The strange thing is, we're just friends, we've kissed just once since our night together, but every time we get together it feels so romantic and sensual. Is that crazy?"

"Not at all. I think you and Ford are in love and have been since February, and you're both forcing yourselves to ignore how you really feel."

"We have to, though," Danica said. "I can't start something with a man who wants a big family when I don't know if I want even one child. So we decided to be friends, but it's hard."

"Can you imagine having a family with Ford?" Candace asked.

"I have thought about it. Last night we went into town with Brandy to pick up toys for Ford's niece and nephew's birthday party, and someone mistook us for a family. I liked it. I felt like I was part of something special."

Candace glanced at Brandy. "Yup, I know exactly what you mean. One minute it was just me, not really connected to anything except scattered relatives I wasn't close to, and suddenly I was someone's mother. The instantaneous bond and connection I felt with Brandy the moment she was born and placed in my arms was the most amazing thing I've ever felt."

"But you didn't necessarily want kids before?" she asked.

"Not really. I didn't think about it. I was focused on trying to get work and trying to find a great guy. I found neither. Like I said, until I was pregnant I had no idea I *wanted* to be."

"It's definitely not coincidence that we both felt the same on the subject," Danica said. "Both not struck by baby fever, I mean."

"Yeah, not coincidence. We were raised in a

pretty cold family with a lot of stupid estrangements. Family has never meant for us what it
seems to for other people."

That struck Danica as so sad that she just sat
glumly staring at her bagel.

"Remember how you wanted *eight* kids when
you were little?" Candace asked on a laugh.

Danica stared at her. "What? I wanted eight
kids?"

"You don't remember? You were seven, I think.
You had lists of name possibilities for all eight
kids. Their names would all start with the letter M, after your best friend, Molly. You had this
black-and-white notebook that you labeled 'Danica's Dreams.' I used to think that was so barfy,
but now it seems really sweet. I think you were
in second grade. I can't believe I remember this
and you don't."

Danica tried to latch on to a memory fighting
to surface, but she couldn't recall saying anything
like that. Her memory of a lot of her childhood was
pretty spotty; the mind had a way of repressing the
bad. She could definitely see planning to name her
children all after Molly, her first real friend. They
were best friends to this day.

"You should look in your old keepsake chest,"

Candace said. "Mom made one for each of us, and she'd put the usual milestone stuff in it."

"Maybe Mom was warmer and fuzzier than I remember? A keepsake chest seems sentimental and sweet."

Candace sipped her coffee and then nodded. "Grandma Eliza bought the chests for her when each of us was born, so it's not like she went out and got them herself. She'd put in old report cards, school stuff, clothing we outgrew but that she liked. I think you have my chest, too."

"I'll look through it later," Danica said. "But I'm sure Mom wouldn't have kept that notebook."

"You never know what you'll find in that old stuff," Candace said.

Old stuff. A chill ran up her spine at the idea of riffling through the past. Danica had always thought it better to follow the old adage to leave well enough alone, but if she wanted to understand herself better, pawing through her past just might be a way.

"Candace?"

Her sister tilted her head.

"Do you think it's the bond with Brandy that's made you so open to finding your Mr. Right after you've been through the wringer?"

"Definitely. I used to date jerks. Now, I want a

good father for Brandy. Someone who'll love us both with everything he is, put us first. But I think that deep down, I really do believe in love and the fairy tale even though I know, from firsthand experience, that there aren't always happy endings. I think it's possible. It's possible for you, too, Dani."

The use of the nickname she'd given up long ago had her all wistful.

"Good," she said. Because she might not know what she wanted, but she wanted to know that love just might conquer all. Even her deepest fears.

In the huge backyard of the main house at the Dawson Family Guest Ranch, full of family, friends and a lot of kids, Ford played soccer with his two-year-old nephew, Danny. The adorable little boy kicked the foam ball right in the goal Ford had declared between his wide spread legs, earning cheers from the crowd. Ford scooped up his nephew, who held his ever-present lovey—a stuffed cape-draped lion named Zul, and ran with him around the yard, chanting "goal, goal, goal."

"Goal!" Danny repeated, flying Zul high over his head.

Ford hugged his nephew tight and set him down, his chest overflowing with love for the little guy. Danny had named the superhero stuffed animal after his own hero, Ford's brother, Axel, before he could actually pronounce Axel. These days, Danny called him Daddy. Axel had married Danny's mother, Sadie, after rescuing Danny, who'd gone missing on a family hike up a mountain. Sadie was expecting their second child soon.

Ford watched as Danny raced over to his father, who hugged him and set him on his shoulders as they both watched the birthday party unfold.

I want that, he thought. *I want my toddler up on my shoulders. Another one pulling at the leg of my pants. Another one in my wife's arms. I want a backyard of littles.*

As he glanced around the party, catching sight of his five siblings with their babies, that feeling was stronger and stronger. He loved this. For so long he'd run from it—from family, from kiddie birthday parties, from the Dawson name here in Bear Ridge. Since he'd been back in town, Bear Ridge didn't remind him of his father or haunting memories that for years had woken him up in the middle of the night, frantic with worry that as the eldest Dawson kid, he'd forgotten one outside, responsible for them all while their father was drunk and out of it. Now, his hometown was only about what he saw in this yard—his siblings, future generations of Dawsons that would grow up proud of who they were. By the buffet table, filled with burgers and hot dogs and fruit and beverages and an incredible assortment of cookies, his brother Noah stood with his wife, Sara, each holding a twin—the birthday duo—and chatting with their sister, Daisy, and her husband, Harrison, who held their baby son, Tony. Sitting down and chomping on burgers piled high with the works were his brothers Rex and Axel, chatting with their nearest neighbors to the west, who had a longtime ranch and had known their grandparents. And over by the huge pile of presents was his brother Zeke and his girlfriend, Molly—

And beside Molly, kneeling down in front of baby Lucy's stroller, was Danica Dunbar.

He did a double take, the sight of her at his family party so unexpected. He wound his way through the crowd. "This is a surprise."

"I got an SOS from Molly," Danica said. "Emergency babysitting pickup."

Zeke leaned close. "One of Molly's cousins is having an emergency appendectomy. We thought we'd just leave Lucy with someone here, but she's been so cranky the past half hour that we figured she'd be better off away from the action. This party just might go on till tomorrow."

Ford smiled. "Probably."

Lucy started shrieking and banging her fists on her little stroller table, her curly hair bouncing in every direction. Ford knelt down, undid her harness and took her out, standing as he cradled her against his chest and rubbed her back. The baby stared at him for a long moment with huge green eyes, then rested her head against his chest and grabbed his ear, her eyes drooping.

"Um, ow," he whispered, smiling at Molly.

"Oh, I forgot to tell you she does that," Zeke said with a grin. "Champion ear grabber. She's never letting go. Sorry."

Ford grinned. "Annabel threw up on me the other day. Trust me, that was worse. Look, you two go ahead. We've got this."

"Oh, we do, do we?" Zeke said, eyebrow raised.

"Danica and I are partners on a town initiative," he said, "so we needed to get together tonight anyway. Everyone knows I'm the baby whisperer of Wyoming."

"I'm definitely not, so I appreciate that he is," Danica said with a smile. "Yeah, you two—go. We'll take good care of Lucy. Good luck to your cousin, Molly."

After explaining what was where in the stroller and diaper bag, the two of them left, and since Lucy started screeching again, Ford said his good-byes to his family, kissed the birthday twins and he and Danica headed out. They'd both parked at the main gate just down the road, so they got Lucy settled in her stroller with a new stuffed animal to clutch, and like magic, she fell asleep by the time they made the walk to the gate.

Ford eyed their cars. "Why don't we take yours? I'll have the rookie drive me over tomorrow morning so I can get my truck."

"Sounds good. Oh, no—Molly and Zeke were going to put one of their car seats in my car, but it slipped our minds."

"No worries—I've got three different car seats in the back of my truck for any little relative or pint-size citizen who might need a lift. I've got it covered."

"I'll just text Molly that so they won't worry," Danica said.

As he lifted the rear-facing seat out of his truck and carried it over to her car, he stopped short and stared just beyond the gates to the wide grassy area on both sides, trees lining the road out of the ranch.

Wait a minute.

Yes.

"You okay?" Danica asked, eyeing him. "You look like you saw a ghost or something."

"I think I did," he said, staring out at the sides of

the road just past the gate. "My dad died two De-
cembers ago. He left me a hand-scrawled map that
he made when he was clearly drunk, and it showed
an area about a half mile out from the barns near
a certain cluster of trees. All this time, my siblings and I have been digging like idiots looking
for what he buried. But I just got socked with this
intense feeling that he buried it out there, just beyond the gates, as if he wanted whatever offended
him in the diary off ranch property."

"What was it he buried?" Danica asked.

"My mother's diary."

"Oh boy," she said. She glanced at Lucy in her
stroller, the baby fast asleep. "Let's take advantage
of her deep sleep and try to find it."

"Yeah?" he asked. "I can come back tomorrow.
We've got Lucy and a pile of matchmaking forms
to go through."

"We're here, and there are two of us. One for
each side of the gate."

He appreciated that. As Danica wheeled the
stroller over to a shady spot under a tree, he tried
to think like his dad. Bo Dawson had found the
diary in the middle of the night, read it, got upset,
got caught with it and had run out of the house
with it, hiding somewhere in the dark until his
wife had given up and gone back inside. Ford could

imagine his father going just past the gate, to the left, where the grassy area was wider and led to the woods. If a car came or his wife's footsteps sounded, he could easily hide between one of the huge tree trunks.

But he would have been drunk, so he wouldn't have gone far. Ford looked over to two big trees just to the left and walked behind them.

"I might be completely off, as I have been for a year and a half. But something tells me this might be the spot. Something feels right."

And wrong. Like maybe he wasn't meant to find the diary. Sometimes he thought his father did such a bad job with the map on purpose. Maybe he wanted to make it impossible for Ford to find the diary to save him from whatever had set Bo off, while at the same time scoring points for at least trying to give Ford something of his mother's history, her thoughts, the truth behind his early childhood.

Ford had no idea what it could be. It had to be something bad.

"As long as I don't find out I'm not really a Dawson, I think I can handle whatever's in there," Ford said, explaining about the night his father buried the book.

Danica grimaced. "Ugh, Ford, maybe you should just leave it buried."

He shrugged, stuffing his hands in his pockets. "My dad wanted me to have it. Sort of. So he was trusting the truth. Maybe. I don't know what the hell I'm talking about."

"Well, if you want to try to find it, I'm your gal. Got a shovel?"

He held up a finger and jogged over to the gatehouse, which was staffed during working hours. There were always a few tools and a first-aid kit in there. He found a shovel—you never could predict April weather in Wyoming—and rushed back over to where Danica stood.

"Here," he said, poking the shovel down into the grassy dirt. "Behind these two trees. Hidden from view of the road both ways."

He poked at the ground for a good ten minutes, every thirty seconds glancing over at Lucy to make sure he hadn't woken her or that she wasn't awake and about to shriek.

"Don't worry about Lucy," Danica said. "If she wakes up, I've got her."

He also appreciated that. Which was funny because he'd actually horned in on her babysitting session.

He struck the ground again and the shovel sank

in. Ford froze, his breath catching. "Oh, man. I just a hit a hole." He looked at Danica, who stared at him wide-eyed, then down at the ground. He shoved out some dirt and dropped to his knees, scooping out more dirt, his knuckles grazing something hard.

Like a metal box.

He reached in and grabbed the edge of it, tilting it until he could finagle it out of the hole on its side. "I can't believe it. I actually found the thing." He stared down at the old fishing tackle box and popped the latch. "Better make sure the diary is actually in here."

Danica wheeled the stroller closer and knelt beside him. He opened the lid. And there in the box was a dark red leather diary, imprinted in gold lettering with the word *Diary* and the year: thirty years ago. Beside it was a bunch of tiny pieces of paper, kind of a pale yellow. Maybe that had been a page Bo Dawson *really* hadn't liked.

Ford closed the lid and shoveled the dirt back in the hole, trying to fill it best he could and then packing it all down hard. They walked back to the gate, Ford returning the shovel to the gatehouse and then meeting Danica by her car. He finally did the transfer of the car seat, got Lucy settled with only the slightest stir, and they both got in.

"Wow," she said.

"Yeah."

"Look, if you want some privacy right now, I can drop you home. We don't need to work on the matchmaking forms tonight."

He wasn't sure if he wanted to be alone with the thing, frankly. "I know it seems crazy, but it took me a long time to come around to even look for the thing. Kept me away from Bear Ridge knowing it was here. I don't know that I'm ready to jump in and actually read it. For now it's enough to know I have it."

"I totally understand that," she said, covering his hand with hers.

He wanted to reach for her so badly, just wrap his arms around her and hold on. But instead he buckled his seat belt.

"Ready?" she asked, turning the ignition.

He really didn't know.

Chapter Eight

Danica glanced at Ford as they arrived at his farmhouse just a few blocks past the center of the town. He'd been quiet on the ride over—understandable—and though he'd shut off the ignition, he didn't otherwise move.

Danica turned toward him. "Like you said, you don't have to read the diary. Right away, anyway. Or ever. You have it, at least."

He nodded, but stared out the window. "For the past year and a half I think I was relieved every time I didn't find it. Who knows what that thing says? My father wasn't easy to offend, so it had to be something bad."

She put her hand on his forearm, and he turned to look at her. She'd never seen him like this. Vulnerable. Unsure. Off balance. If only she could put her arms around him. A *friend* could do that, but there was just too much in the air between them to pretend they were just friends.

"Well, let's get this very cute baby to bed," he said. "I made a nursery in one of the bedrooms so I'd always have space for my little relatives. Oh, wait, you know that. You were at my housewarming party." He glanced at her, and clearly even the thought of their day and night together couldn't lift his heavy heart. He cleared his throat. "Anyway, Lucy will want for nothing."

He turned to smile at Lucy, but she was rear-facing, and all they both got was a view of the back of the car seat. His shoulders slumped.

I want to give you everything, she thought out of nowhere. *You're so thoughtful and good. So damned gorgeous. I want you to have everything you want.*

She suddenly pictured herself giving a gentle push to that tire swing hanging off the oak tree in the front yard, their little one belly down, arms and legs dangling, happy squeals and shouts of "higher, faster" called at her. Ford was right there, too, giving a monster push, then he scooped their child from the swing and put him on his shoulders—ah, it was a boy—and they took a walk down to the creek in the backyard to look for frogs.

The images filled her heart instead of freezing it. Made her feel…tingly.

It's probably the right husband who'll turn your head and heart around about the idea of having children, she remembered Molly saying when Danica had finally opened up to her about her ambivalence about having kids. *Of course, it's totally possible that you just don't want kids and that's absolutely fine. But your Mr. Right will be the one who makes everything feel right, Danica. Kids in your future or no kids.*

Anyway, the feeling and those images of herself as a mother and Ford as the father were brand-new and tentative, and she'd keep it to herself while it blossomed…or didn't. Maybe she was reacting to Ford being all vulnerable in front of her. Or maybe something inside her was beginning to shift. Because of Ford. Because of Candace being home. Because of helping care for her baby niece.

Ford took Lucy from her car seat and handed her to Danica, the baby stirring slightly. Danica gently caressed her back and slightly rocked her, and she immediately settled down. *Stop trying to make this easy for me*, she thought with a smile.

I'm still scared to death about the idea of being a mother. But I can imagine it. And that was something she'd never experienced before. With her ex-husband, she *hadn't* been able to imagine it.

As they headed up the blue stone walkway, they passed the tire swing and she felt the tiniest thrill. Danica had a secret; for once, a secret that was hers alone and felt good to have and keep.

The moment Danica came through the door, she was hit by memories. She'd loved this house from the moment it had come on the market, and when she'd met Ford and heard what he was looking for in a home, she knew this was the one. The three acres of land, the pristine white farmhouse with its wraparound porch, managing to seem ancient and modern at the same time, the woods and creek at the far end of the backyard. Inside was gorgeous, too. A big country kitchen with state-of-the-art appliances, a huge living room with a dark-wood-beamed ceiling and a river rock fireplace that practically took up an entire wall. When she'd been his Realtor, he'd only mentioned that he was single now but wanted a house in case he "ever did get himself married," and she'd been charmed by that. She'd felt included, crazy as that sounded, as if someone felt the same way she did—single, but you never knew what the future held. But then the night of his housewarming party, he seemed to know exactly what he wanted his future to hold. He'd only been back in Bear Ridge a short time then, but maybe the town and his family had worked their magic on him.

Maybe he'd work his magic on her and she'd want the unexpected, too. That little picture she'd had just a little while ago in his car certainly made it seem possible.

He took the car seat from her to carry Lucy upstairs, and she trailed behind him. In the nursery, he held the carrier up for her to unclick the harness, and she took out the baby, then set her down gently. She stirred again, her arm quivering a bit before shooting up near her head. Success.

"Hey, I'm getting pretty good at this," she said with a smile. She stared down at beautiful Lucy, all those curls like her mommy's, and the slightest pitter-patter thrummed in her chest. "My sister told me that when I was little, like sevenish, she remembered me saying I was going to have eight kids and give them all names starting with *M* after my new best friend Molly. I can't remember that at all. Isn't that strange?"

He tilted his head. "Not strange, actually. There's a lot of my childhood I've forgotten. Noah and Daisy will start up a 'remember when' and I don't—even though I say I was definitely there. From the innocuous to the rough."

She bit her lip and nodded. "Well, when I was seven, I also wanted to be a princess and an astronaut and a puppy, so I won't put too much stock in saying I wanted eight kids." She tried to add a laugh, but it wouldn't come out. If that want had been in her once, maybe her upbringing, the coldness, the estrangement of aunts and grandfathers who'd simply walked out decades ago had seeped into her bones and cells, and the whole concept of family had felt like something scary instead of warm and comforting. Maybe that was why she couldn't remember about the eight kids. Candace probably didn't remember some old childhood dreams of her own, either.

"Lucy is one lucky little girl," Danica whispered. "Best mom in the world. And since Molly and your brother are so hot and heavy, it looks like she might soon get an amazing stepdaddy too."

"They do seem very serious," Ford said. "It's wild how the family you end up with can dictate your whole life. Or try to. Mine had a hold over me for far too long."

Did hers? How could she be sure her upbringing was the reason behind her disinterest in having kids? Didn't some women just not want children?

Not everything had to be rooted in how a person was raised.

"I think mine has, too," she said. "I don't know. Big questions that I don't love thinking about."

"I know how that goes. Story of my life. It's why I'm gonna keep that diary in the box forever probably. Does that sound nuts?"

"It's hard to say whether you should read it or not. On one hand, it's your mother's private journal. Her thoughts. It was wrong of your father to read it, let alone hide it from her. But both your parents are gone and you do have questions about what broke up their marriage, what got your dad upset enough to bury the diary. Maybe you're right that reading it will bring some closure."

"If not exactly peace," he said.

She nodded. "Or maybe…"

"Or maybe I'll get the opposite of peace and therefore no closure."

She let out a sigh. "Easier question is—are you hungry? I can root around your kitchen, which I still know like the back of my hand, and whip us up something."

"I had two burgers and a hot dog and a ton of pasta salad. I'm done eating for days."

"I'm pretty full, too," she said. "How about coffee?"

He nodded. "I'm on it. And let's make some matches. I need to clear my head, think about something other than the diary." He got up and headed into the kitchen. She grabbed her folder of matchmaking request forms that she'd brought in from the car and sat back down on the couch.

By the time he returned with two cups of coffee on a tray with cream and sugar, she'd found two matches for Stella Winkler, who worked in the bakery, one for a rancher named Henry Cowler, and three for Ethan Gawlings, a sixty-four-year-old retired widower looking for a movie companion.

"I'm on a roll," she said, looking up at Ford as he set down the tray. "Sixty-three-year-old Lila Gomez has been widowed for five years and is finally ready to go on a first date since she was twenty and married her first love. I found her one match, and I'm hoping for a second in case Ethan Gawlings doesn't work out."

Ford sat down and slid the tray over to her. "Hey, I know Ethan. He started an animal sanctuary that his son and daughter-in-law now run. He took in injured or unwanted farm animals and let them live out their golden years in peace."

"That's very sweet," Danica said, adding cream and sugar to her mug.

Ford added cream to his own mug and took a

long sip. "Let's get to it." He opened his folder and got busy, but Danica would catch him staring out the window time and again. He did manage to find four matches in an hour—Danica had found matches, and multiples in many cases, for fifteen. By the time Molly and Zeke arrived to pick up Lucy, who had slept like a champ the entire time, Ford seemed weary, like the weight of Wyoming was on his shoulders.

After Molly and Zeke left with Lucy, Danica packed up her folder, including the matches Ford had made, and headed to the door.

"If you need an ear, mine's available," she said.

"I appreciate that." He opened the door, the pink-and-orange setting sun so beautiful in the distance.

She didn't want to go. She wanted to give him privacy with his thoughts, to mull over what he wanted to do about the diary, but she would have to force herself out the door. "Well, bye."

"I'll text you about another matchmaking night," he said, and then suddenly reached out his hand.

She took it and wrapped her arms around him, and he pulled her close.

Danica closed her eyes, reveling in the feel of him against her, his strong chest, the scent of his soap and shampoo. She glanced up at him, and he touched her face, and then suddenly they were kissing, his arms tightening around her, one hand winding its way in her hair. Her legs were all wobbly.

"I didn't intend on that," he said. But he didn't step back.

"Me neither." *And I want more.*

But suddenly the wobbly got to her head, and she was so unsure of what was going on with them, whether this was playing with fire. It felt like it.

"I'd better get going," she said. "See you soon."

"Night, Danica."

She stepped out into the sunset, knowing she was leaving her heart behind.

If Danica hadn't left when she had, Ford would have picked her up, kicked the door shut with his foot and carried her upstairs to his bed. Good thing she was thinking straight because he sure wasn't. The combination of her nearness, how understanding she'd been of his mood, that she'd been there when he'd found the diary, and how damned attracted he was to her had had a powerful grip on him. What he would give for a repeat of two months ago, though this time without any conversation to send her fleeing, so he could be with her, lose himself, forget. But she *had* left, wisely.

After a long, hot shower, he headed down to the kitchen for yet another mug of strong coffee, the tackle box in front of him on the table, lid open, the diary and its ripped-up page right there. "What the hell do you say?" He asked it aloud, then realized he was losing it and grabbed his phone to punch in a group text to his siblings.

Found the diary when I was leaving the ranch today. Had a lightbulb moment that Dad might have buried it right outside the gates to "rid the property of it." I was right. Haven't cracked it open. Might not.

Ping. Daisy: Holy cannoli, Ford. You okay? I can come over with the really good Hungarian mushroom soup I just made.

Ping. Rex: Damn. You gonna read it? I don't know if I would.

Ping. Axel: What Rex said.

Ping. Zeke: Read the first couple of lines, then decide if you can KEEP reading. Good luck, bro.

Ping. Daisy: I like Zeke's advice.

Ping. Noah: What Daisy said. Otherwise it'll eat you alive and you won't be able to think of anything else.

Ping. Rex: Let us know when you want to talk.

He texted back: Will do. Thanks, guys. I'll take a rain check on that soup, Daisy.

He put down the phone, took another slug of coffee and picked up the diary. It didn't burn his hands or make him explode like he almost thought it would.

He *could* read the first few lines. Just to see.

Thirty years old. He shook his head, trying to remember back to being four, but everything was a jumble. He flipped through the diary without actually reading anything. He could see his mother's handwriting, sometimes blue ink, sometimes black, pencil now and again. Toward the end there was a page ripped out jaggedly. He glanced in the box and the matching ripped-up pieces. Whatever had been on that page had sent Bo Dawson into a tailspin.

Okay, he thought, finishing the coffee. *Here goes everything.* He opened the diary to the first page. It wasn't January 1, as most diaries began; the page was dated May 2. His mother wrote about confiding her troubles to a friend, who'd suggested she get it out in a journal. Ellen Dawson had never kept a diary and wanted one, the old-fashioned kind with a lock and key, but she'd only found this one in three colors at the drugstore and so had bought it.

Maybe she'd go on about the different colors available. What else she'd bought in the drugstore. If she'd run into a neighbor. He'd like to read all that everyday stuff. Not what was surely about to follow.

Ford was pretty sure he knew what his mother's troubles had been. An alcoholic husband with a wandering eye who was slowly destroying the ranch. That was common knowledge. The next paragraph was about two of the cows going missing, and Bo saying they'd gone off in the direction of Clover Mountain. *He's drunk right now. Though when is he not?* she'd written. *How could the cows have wandered off out of sight without either the foreman or their two last ranch hands noticing? I have a terrible feeling that Bo is sneaking the animals off the ranch for drinking and gambling money. I hate thinking this way—this ranch is our future, our son's future, and Bo's family legacy. But come on. Last week, two goats mysteriously disappeared. Now two huge cows.*

There were pages of this kind of thing. Ford sat at the table, his shoulders relaxing a bit. This wasn't anything new or unexpected. He could deal with this. Zeke's advice, siblings-approved, to read the first page and see if he could go on was solid.

Of course he wasn't anywhere near the ripped-out page. If things were starting to get bad for his mother on page one, things had to be plenty bad that close to the nearly full diary.

He didn't have to read far.

May 8. I saw Bo kissing a woman—and I'm talking tongue down the throat, hand in the bleached blond curls—just down the little alley between the pizza place and the office building. For all that bastard knew I could have been driving past with our son. He knows I like to go into town at least once a day. Thank God I was alone. I pulled over to the side of the road and cried hard for a good fifteen minutes. What am I going to do? This isn't how it was supposed to be. I want better for myself, and I want everything for Ford. What the hell am I gonna do?

Ford's shoulders were back to tense, bunched-up rocks again.

Oh, Mom, he thought, his heart breaking for her. She'd been a good mother, kind, loving, nurturing. But as a divorced parent with an ex who drank and gambled his depleting income away, she'd had to work long hours to make ends meet. She'd been a typist for two lawyers in town, and

they'd encouraged her to get her paralegal certificate, which meant reluctantly dropping him
at his negligent dad's for her night classes three
times a week. But Bo had remarried the minute
the ink had dried on their divorce papers, a baby
already on the way—Axel. Ford had liked his stepmother, but his mother had tried to warn her, and
Diana Dawson, who was apparently madly in love
with her husband, didn't want to hear it. The two
women barely got along. Once his mother had become a paralegal, Bo had only seen his dad every
other weekend for a while.

He'd admired his mother. And to read of her
heartbreak at the hands of his father...

He shut the diary, dumped it in the box and
closed the lid, stalking around the kitchen. Maybe
he'd read enough. Drinking, gambling, cheating,
his mother sobbing on the side of the road in her
car. Broke, with a young son to raise.

Every reason he'd ever had for not wanting
to marry or have kids came surging back into
his cells. Danica had the right idea. He'd had the
right idea until so much time away from his old
memories had made him forget, made him soft.

Six kids? No. He was just fine on his own,

where no one got hurt, no one got disappointed, and no one cried on the side of the road because of him.

Chapter Nine

On Sunday morning, 5:07 a.m., Danica yawned and hurried into Brandy's nursery so that the little screecher wouldn't wake up her mother. Candace had come home late, and Danica had poked her head out of her room to check in. Her sister's moony smile told her she'd had a wonderful time on her long date with Jasper.

Danica dashed over to the crib, Brandy letting out sharp little cries and waving her fists. She lifted the baby out, Brandy liking that and immediately piping down, her big blue eyes on Danica. "You are such a marvel," Danica whispered. "Look

at you. A tiny human, the entire world open before you, everything to learn, everything to know."

She held Brandy against her for a moment, rel-
ishing the warm, solid weight of her in her arms.
She loved the baby shampoo scent, her soft fleece
yellow-and-white footie pj's with the little brown
buffalos charging across the yellow stripes. "Let's
get you changed and into a cute little outfit, then
we'll go have breakfast. Sound good?"

Brandy reached up and grabbed the side of Danica's jaw.

Danica laughed. "Guess it does!"

After getting Brandy changed, Danica held the
baby while she poked through the baby's clothes.
She gasped happily at the sight of a white fleece
shirt, "Awesome Niece" embroidered with tiny
blue stars across the front. Beneath it were the
matching little fleece stretchy pants. And in the
drawer with the diapers and socks, Danica found
the collection of socks and baby booties she'd sent,
a package arriving for her sister just about every
month since Brandy was born. Candace might not
have been open to her sister visiting, but that didn't
mean Danica couldn't show she cared, that she
was thinking of her sister and niece. She changed
Brandy into the cute outfit, then snuggled her
against her chest and kissed the top of her head.

"Let's go have breakfast, cutie. And then I need at least two cups of coffee."

As she gave Brandy's soft cheek a gentle caress, she was gripped by *I want*.

There it was again. I want.

A baby? A Brandy of her own?

She grinned and gave a little spin, holding Brandy in the air. "What have you done to me, baby girl? Suddenly I'm thinking I want my own little one?"

A warm burst of gooey something spread in her chest, and she cuddled Brandy against her and then headed downstairs, wondering if the feeling would follow her around. It did.

Maybe it's Ford, she thought. Like Molly said— maybe when you fall for someone for all the right reasons, you stop being scared for the wrong reasons.

She really had no idea and wasn't interested in analyzing it too closely. For now, that these pops of feeling, of want, of what seemed to be maternal urges were happening inside her was enough. She thought back to picturing herself and Ford swinging their toddler on the tire in his yard.

Maybe I'm changing, Brandy, she thought as she put the baby in the playpen in the kitchen while she made up a bottle. A few minutes later, she sat down at the kitchen table with the beautiful view of spring flowers she'd spent a fortune on for the porch, Brandy nestled in her arms as she took her bottle. *Maybe everything that's had a grip on me the past year since my divorce is finally letting go.*

All she knew for sure was that it felt good. And that she couldn't wait to see Ford again.

Maybe they could be a perfect match, after all.

Ford knelt in front of the Lexus's slashed rear tires and took some photos with his phone, zooming in on the note that was stabbed into the slashed area with a long nail: LOL. It was almost five in the afternoon on Sunday, and Ford was on his sixth revenge-crime of the day. Dating and breakups were bringing out the worst in residents of Bear Ridge. His brother Rex had taken the rookie up and down the block and across the street to look for evidence, whether fast getaway tire tracks, a receipt that had dropped out of a pocket, chewed gum, a cigarette butt, even a wallet or cell phone. Some bad guys weren't very bright and dropped their IDs.

"I want whoever did this prosecuted to the full extent of the law!" Ethan Stutley all but shouted, pointing at the tires. Tall and imposing, but neither taller nor more imposing than Ford at six-two and solid muscle, Ethan was in his early forties with white-blond hair and ice-blue eyes. He wore square silver-framed glasses and a business suit. Ethan was a CPA with his own shingle on Main Street. Ford knew him from the town basketball league. Ethan got many fouls.

"Understood," Ford said. "Given that your and your neighbor's video camera didn't pick up the perpetrator's face or any identifying details, this won't be an easy case to solve. My rookie has dusted for prints, so we'll see if anything pops up there. But I'll tell you, Ethan. People who pull this kind of crap will likely make themselves known. Brag about it to someone who gossips, or he or she will try to do something else and be caught in the act. They'll think they've gotten away with this and it won't be enough."

Ethan nodded, calming down some. "I'm installing another camera from the front yard, so hopefully that'll catch the scumbucket." He extended his hand. "Thanks for coming out, Ford. Appreciate it."

Ford shook his hand. "I'll let you know if the fingerprints are a match."

Unfortunately for Ethan, he wasn't very well liked around town. He was a complainer, called the cops on dogs that barked too long or about teens congregating near his house. He told loud talkers on cell phones to shut the hell up already, though some people appreciated that he did that. He was divorced and had filled out a matchmaking profile—before Ford had joined the team—and had been doing a lot of dating. For the past week he'd been seeing one woman, and Ford wouldn't be surprised if someone didn't like that, for reasons myriad and varied.

As Ethan headed inside his house, Rex and the rookie were back. The rookie carried an evidence bag containing a gross wad of gum.

"We found only this," Dylan said.

Ford nodded. "Like I told Ethan, the perp will probably make another move and mess up and get caught. We'll get him eventually."

"These revenge calls are driving me nuts," Rex said, taking off his officer's hat and running a hand through his dark hair. "The relationship didn't work out. Move on, people."

"Yoo-hoo, officers!"

Ford turned to see Mayor Abbott calling out her open car window as she was driving toward them. She pulled against the curb and came rushing over, a flurry of fast activity, as always.

"A favor, if I may?" she asked, looking at all three of them but focusing on Ford. Uh-oh.

"What can we do for you, Pauline?" Ford asked,

"Well, I heard about Ethan Stutley's slashed tires," she said, then leaned closer and added, "though that might not be matchmaking-dating related at all. I mean, the man makes enemies while waiting for his coffee order at Java Joe's." She shook her head. "And there were two other incidents this morning, weren't there? Can you believe someone untied Jennifer Sabu's French bulldog from the post in front of the bakery and just left the leash on the sidewalk? Someone wanted that dog to run away! He could have been hit by a car." She shook her head again.

Luckily, Banjo had stayed put, refusing to budge until he saw his owner walk out of the bakery.

"So I was thinking," the mayor continued. "I'm going to announce that these crimes will not be tolerated and that our matchmaking initiative is being put to an end because of a few bad apples. Our speed dating event will be canceled unless, between now and next week, there is not a single crime related to someone being pissed off about someone dating someone else."

"Sounds good to me," Ford said, Rex and rookie Dylan nodding.

"And about that favor," she said. "I'd like you to give a talk to the entire town. An actual emergency town meeting to discuss what's going on. People like and respect you, Ford. You're the law *and* you're single. You're right out there with the daters, as far as they know. I think you'll have more of an impact than me or the chief."

Ford mulled it over for a second. "I don't know that a lecture on right and wrong is going to get through to the perpetrators, though."

"Agreed. Your uniform will speak to and for the right and wrong. You want to talk about why the revenge crimes should end, why those committing the acts need to shift their mindset. There's someone for everyone in Bear Ridge, and no one needs to get so upset over an ex dating someone new that they unleash someone's dog on a post."

Ah. He got it. She wanted him to come from the human angle. The heart.

"I think it's a great idea," Rex said. "We should probably incentivize people to show up—the ones who need to listen most, I mean."

"Oh, I thought of that," Pauline said. "Trust me, I think of everything."

She wasn't kidding. Pauline Abbott was a one-woman powerhouse, and she'd likely one day be governor of Wyoming.

"We'll advertise through word of mouth and on social media that any Bear Ridge resident who attends the talk will receive free admittance to the speed dating event, which otherwise will be twenty-five dollars. If we're forced to cancel that event, the offer is null and void."

"Smart deal," Ford said. "The perpetrators are most likely still single and will want to attend the speed dating event—and for free." Though, of course, there was one eighty-four-year-old wedding-dress thief who broke that mold.

"This Thursday at seven at the town hall?" she asked. "I think we'll have around two hundred attendees. We'll use the large meeting room."

"I'll be there and prepared," he said.

"Knew I could count on you, Detective," she said, patting his arm. She nodded at Rex and Dylan and then dashed back to her car.

The three drove back to the PD, Dylan rushing in to attend a training session with the chief.

"So did you read any of the diary?" Rex asked, turning to glance at Ford as they both got out of his vehicle.

"I read enough to feel like hell," Ford said. "And I only got two pages in."

"Oh, damn. Sorry. Though I guess that was expected, given that Dad stole the diary and buried it."

Ford nodded. "He tore out the most offending

page and dropped the tiny bits of ripped-up page in the tackle box with the diary. So I won't know what that says. Unless maybe there's some context in the pages leading up to it."

"You gonna bother?" Rex asked. "I don't know if I would. Could just make you more unsettled."

"Well, the worst thing I can find out is that I'm not a Dawson, right? That my mother had an affair and I'm someone else's kid, which would open up another whole stinking can of worms. But I look just like the rest of you—and we all got Dad's strong coloring and features."

"Good point. You do have my same good looks."

Ford gave his brother a playful punch on the arm. "So what then? What could she have written that had him so upset he'd bury the thing? I can't come up with much that seems bad enough. I mean, what could possibly offend Bo Dawson to that degree?"

"Yeah, I know what you mean. He was hard to upset unless you got in the way of his booze or persisted in calling him out on it. He'd take that for a good long time before he'd lash out."

"Well, given that this is all in my head now, I have to deal with it instead of just trying to forget about it."

"I'm with you on dealing, Ford. The ostrich approach always backfires."

Yeah, it did.

His phone pinged with a text, and Rex clapped a hand on his shoulder. "I'll head in. Here if you need me. We all are."

"I know. And thanks."

He watched his brother walk into the PD, grateful for all the Dawsons, then looked down at his phone. Danica.

Team Matchmakers are on hiatus? Just when I was getting the hang of it.

He texted back: Hopefully we'll be back up and running soon. The mayor asked me to give the town a heart to heart to try to get the vengefully scored to change their ways.

If anyone can, it's you. After all, you're helping turn me around...

He stared at that last text, wondering what she meant.

In fact, I'd like to take you out on a date, Ford Dawson. I hear the steaks at the Bear Ridge Inn are incredible...

He swallowed. Oh, hell. By "helping turn me around," was she talking about wanting a family? Why else would she suddenly ask him out on a date when they were not dating because she didn't want kids and he did.

Except now he had no interest in marriage or family.

Again, oh, hell.

How was he going to respond to this?

Chapter Ten

While her sister poked around Danica's closet for "the perfect dress to wear for her date with the perfect man" that night, Danica kept staring at her phone, waiting for Ford's response.

Nothing.

Five minutes later, still nothing.

By the time Candace had found a dress, shoes, accessories, and had tried everything on, there was still nothing but radio silence from the detective.

Danica's heart dropped. Maybe she'd been too cryptic with the "you're helping turn me around." Was it possible he didn't know what she meant even after asking him out on a date? He knew why they *weren't* dating. So he had to know what she'd been referring to.

She'd felt so vulnerable typing that, putting it out there, especially to the man himself. The thought of her feeling maternal stirrings was such a big deal to Danica and she'd been so sure he'd respond with a "pick you up at 7" or "I'm coming over right now" and a heart emoji—something—but the moments were ticking by and her phone screen was glaringly empty.

She let out a sigh.

"Uh-oh," Candace said, stopping half-turned in the full-length mirror on her closet door. "What's that sigh about? You're not mad about me borrowing this incredible dress, are you?"

"No, of course not. And it looks amazing on you. The shoes, too."

Candace tilted her head. "Then what's wrong?"

"I asked Ford out—granted, via text—and he hasn't responded." They weren't even dating and it was hell already.

"Danica, you know that man is crazy about you. I know it and I just got here. If he didn't respond, it's because he's chasing down a suspect or got called into a meeting. Come on."

Maybe. "Or he's not interested in me that way anymore."

"Look at you," Candace said, moving out of the way of the mirror so that Danica could see her reflection from the bed. "You're stunning. Easily the most beautiful woman in this town."

Danica looked at herself. Hair in a messy bun high on her head so her niece's little hands couldn't yank. No makeup. A long-sleeved T-shirt and yoga pants. The old Danica would have looked like this only to go jogging or to deep clean her kitchen. She liked this new Danica, though. Natural. The real her. She'd had no idea she'd been hiding behind two hours of makeup application and hair styling until she went bare. Exposed. Her look had become her identity instead of her personality and character.

Danica shook her head. "Looks might lure someone, but like Mom used to say, pretty is as pretty does. It's far from important. Connecting with someone is about what's in here," she said, touching her chest. "It's about chemistry."

"Ugh, I hated when Mom or Dad would say that to me. They'd both say it with such disdain whenever we made the slightest misstep."

Danica remembered. "I used to be so focused on my appearance. And, yeah, for work I'll still dress up and go in polished because I'm still that woman, too. But I like this natural look. It feels right. It feels like I'm shedding something and becoming who I really am. Does that sound all new agey?"

"No. I get it."

"I used to think all I had was my looks. But between you being here and my getting to bond with Brandy, I've discovered how much family—you guys—really mean to me. I was so afraid of the word *family* for so long. And now I'm not. To the point that I think I can see having a baby of my own, Candace."

Her sister gasped and rushed over to her, squeezing her into a hug. "That's really wonderful. Neither of us is being held to old crud or patterns or beliefs that have nothing to do with who we want to be."

"Yeah!" Danica said. "Team Dunbar—*our* way, *our* version!"

The doorbell rang, and Candace grinned. "There's my hot date. We'll talk tomorrow over breakfast?"

Danica nodded. "Have a great time. You look amazing."

Candace grinned, slipped on Danica's lightweight shiny black trench coat and left in a haze of perfume-scented air.

Danica walked over to the mirror and peered at herself. "Who *we* want to be is right. I decide that. Not my parents or how I was raised or old fears. I decide."

Ping.

She eyed her phone on her bed. Forty-five minutes after her text, he'd finally responded?

She grabbed the phone.

He'd texted: Free right now to talk?

Oh, phooey. This didn't sound good.

Sure. Babysitting but Brandy is asleep. Come on over.

She went downstairs to pace. And wait.

Ford pulled into Danica's driveway, cutting the engine but not moving. He didn't want to deal with this at all, didn't want to talk to her about this, didn't want to disappoint her, hurt her. Once again, they were on different pages.

He forced himself out of the car and knocked on the door.

When she opened it, as usual the sight of her stole his breath for a moment.

"So our timing is once again all wrong?" she asked.

He loved this about her. Getting right to it, putting it out there. Asking the question.

He stepped inside, shutting the door behind

him, and followed her into the living room. She sat on the edge of the sofa, so he stood, hands jammed in his pockets. "Yeah," he finally said. "Yesterday, I would have jumped at the chance to take you out for an amazing night. And now. Everything's just..." He trailed off, not sure what the right term was. *Dead inside? Festering?*

She tilted her head and looked at him. "Just..."

"I thought I'd changed, but it turns out I haven't. Marriage, kids—" He shook his head. "Not in my future. I need to just be on my own, like I've always been."

Danica stared at him. "What—" She stopped, understanding dawning in her eyes. "Oh, Ford. You read your mother's diary."

"Just a few pages. And trust me, those were enough to remind me how easy it is to rip apart a family, bring people you supposedly care about to their knees. I don't want any part of that."

He moved over to the windows and stared out. "You know how you said everything in you froze when I said I wanted six kids? That's how I feel now. Like everything in me froze when I read those pages."

He turned to look at her. Her expression killed him. Concern, regret, despair, maybe even horror. "There are some great men out there, Danica.

Men looking for everything you are. Match yourself with someone who deserves you."

She seemed about to say something and then didn't, until he started walking to the door and touched the doorknob.

She sprang up. "Ford, I understand why the diary got to you so deeply. Based on what you've told me about your parents' marriage, it must have been terribly heartbreaking to read her words. But I think this is going to be a process—not easy, maybe long—as you work through how you feel about it. It doesn't have to change your dreams for yourself."

"Well, it did," he said. "I need to get going."

She came up to him, standing just an inch away, and brought her hands up to either side of his face. "I care about you, Ford."

He moved his own hands to her face and kissed her so deeply that her legs shook. "I care about you, too. Which is why I'm going now."

And with that, he turned and left, his heart clenching.

Danica spent the next couple days with Candace and Brandy, special time with her sister and niece helping to keep her mind off Ford Dawson, and babysitting duty reinforcing that these new feelings she was having about being a mother were very real. Ford hadn't been in contact, and she'd wanted so badly to hear his voice that she'd forced herself just to give him space by merely sending him a quick text: I'm here for you as a friend, just know that.

He'd texted back: Appreciate that. And ditto. I mean it.

So they were friends. Again. As if she could possibly look at any other man in this town and think of him romantically when she'd fallen in love with Ford Dawson. And she had, of that there was no doubt.

Now, Thursday morning, she was back at her desk at the realty office with a busy day of showings. As she'd gotten ready for work, she'd found herself toning down her usual routine. Her skin care regimen she'd never veer from, but did she need a foundation primer, liquid foundation, powder to set it, then a setting spray? She'd used a tinted moisturizer, a touch of blush, a little mascara and her favorite lipstick. This would have been her look for visiting a farm or waiting to have the oil changed in her car. Now it was her new work look, and she liked it. Her hair, too, hadn't been flat ironed and then curled into beachy waves, artfully arranged and sprayed. She'd just added a little gel, blown it dry and put it into a low ponytail. Now that she'd gotten used to having her hair out of her way, she liked that, too.

Expecting a young couple at nine, she glanced at her watch. Twentysomething firefighter Matthew McHaul had made an appointment last week, noting he and his fiancée were just starting the process of looking for a home together. When the door jangled, she glanced over and saw a couple coming in. She heard the tall blond man tell the receptionist they were there to meet with Danica.

She walked over, hand extended. "Hello, welcome to Bear Ridge Realty. I'm Danica Dunbar. It's a pleasure to meet you both."

Matthew introduced himself, then his fiancée. "And this is Lauren Anderson. As I mentioned on the phone last week, we're recently engaged and looking for a house. But we're not sure what we want."

Danica fussed over Lauren's gorgeous round diamond ring as she shook her hand. "Well, let's sit down and get started on finding out what that is." Once the couple was seated at Danica's desk, coffee in front of them, she got out her tablet and electronic pen. "Let's start with what type of property you're interested in. Bear Ridge has so many different types, from condo developments right here off Main Street to single family homes."

"We're looking for a cozy single family house." She gave a price range and Danica entered it into their file info. "Small but at least three bedrooms—one for us, one for a nursery, and one for a guest room for our parents to stay over when our little guy is born." She patted her belly.

"Oh!" Danica said. "Are congratulations in order?"

Matthew grinned and nodded. "Due in November."

"Congratulations!" Danica said. *You are so lucky*, she wanted to say.

And that was a first. She'd never gotten envious about someone announcing a pregnancy before. But as Lauren told a sweet story about how every first baby in their family was a girl and that was how they knew they were having a boy, because they both marched to their own drummers, Danica was aware of how happily jealous she was. *I want to be pregnant and planning the rest of my life with the man I love*, she thought. *Buying a house that's just right for us*.

"I know four off the top of my head that you might love," Danica said. "Within your price range. A couple don't have updated kitchens but they do have tons of charm and character. Let's see those four and go from there. Maybe you'll find your dream home today. Or maybe you'll discover you want more this and less that, less this and more that."

"I'm so excited!" Lauren said, standing up.

Matthew grinned at her and took her hand.

I want what you have, Danica thought again. And I didn't get all the way to this point so that Ford Dawson could do his own one-eighty—for reasons that had and would continue to make him miserable. He was her dream man and if she wanted a future with him, she'd have to help him see he could have it all—the family he'd discovered he wanted *and* peace with his past.

The thing was, Danica had come to this point organically, and Ford would have to, as well. Talking wasn't the way. *Showing* was. And showing was what Danica Dunbar did best.

Chapter Eleven

Mayor Abbott had been right about the large number of attendees for Ford's talk about the "vengeance crimes" Thursday night at the town hall. Promised free admittance to the speed dating event—if good behavior would allow it to be held—222 singles had crowded into the large conference room. Lemonade and doughnut holes, made by the Bear Ridge Cares Society, in abundance on a back table as people came in, were now almost gone. He didn't love the idea of the perpetrators, particularly of the more serious crimes, enjoying refreshments on his time, but he had a good feeling about this plan working.

Ford stood at the front of the room, microphone in hand, slowly moving from one side to the other and back, making eye contact. He wore his uniform, which was navy blue with silver patches, and his hat, which he'd take off when he got started. He'd spent just about all his spare time the past few days working on what he'd say, going over lines in his head, fine-tuning. It helped keep his mind off the diary, and off Danica and how he'd very likely blindsided her the other day. He felt like hell about that. He'd taken her beautiful, tentative step toward a whole new future and turned his back on her—as a potential partner, anyway. He'd made it clear he would always be her friend. That didn't make him feel better, though.

He glanced at the big analog clock on the wall. A minute till seven o'clock. He'd start on time, knowing that perps either came at the appointed hour or a few minutes late. The door opened and a few people came in. Including Danica. She smiled at him and he found himself giving a tight smile back, which made her smile fade.

Exactly what he didn't want to happen was happening. He was affecting her, causing her grief by just being himself. By being tied in knots over the diary and everything he was, everything his parents had been.

The second hand moved to the twelve. Showtime.

He introduced himself, welcomed the audience, and was about to start talking when the door opened and a few more people came in. He noted Andrew Morton going to the back wall to grab an unfolded chair and make his own last row. A ranch hand. Andrew didn't have a record, but Ford had cited him for "making a disturbance," after a fight almost broke out in front of the one bar in town. Andrew apparently hadn't liked seeing a woman he'd briefly dated leaving with someone else, and they'd had words, but someone had called police before a punch could be thrown. He'd happened to catch Andrew driving a couple times in town and kept an eye on him, but the guy hadn't committed any crimes.

"Dating. Romance. Relationships. Weddings," Ford began. "That's what's supposed to be up in Bear Ridge. Instead, crime is up. Forty-two percent in a month. This is our town. It belongs to all of us. And when someone's tires are slashed, when someone's dog is let loose from a post, when rotten eggs are thrown at someone's car windows, that's against all of us. I'm here to tell you that the revenge crimes have to stop."

He glanced around, taking in the nods and mur-

murings, and a few shouts of "That's right. You tell 'em, Detective Dawson."

"Look, I'm a single guy," he continued. "I know dating can be rough. And I know firsthand that getting dumped hurts. I know how hard it is to see someone you may still have feelings for with someone new. One of the reasons why I left Casper two months ago to move back to my hometown and join the police force was because a relationship fell apart. So, yeah, I know how it feels. But I also know that when you're down-and-out over something not working out, the answer isn't lashing out at either the person who hurt you or a new person in their life. That's about revenge. But that's unfair. How many of you in this room have broken up with someone because it just wasn't working out, didn't feel right, wasn't moving forward, didn't make you happy, or yes, because you met someone else and wanted to pursue a relationship with that person? How many?"

Just about every hand went up. Including Andrew Morton's. Including Ford's. And Danica's.

"Exactly," he said. "We've all been the ones to end a relationship. And we've all had it done to us. So if you're upset, if you're thinking, I know what will make me better—I'm going to throw a brick through my ex's window—I'm asking you not to.

I'm asking you to let it go, let that person go. And use your energy to find the right person. That's what it's about. That's what we all want. It's what this whole matchmaking initiative is about, it's what the speed dating event is about—if we can still hold it. If there's even one revenge crime in the next few days, the event will be canceled. I'm asking for all y'alls' support here. And I'm going to offer up mine. If you're feeling out of sorts over a relationship not working out and you could use a friend, someone to talk to in confidence, come see me at the PD or call me on my cell." He read out the number, hoping he wouldn't regret that with prank texts and calls. "Thank you."

There were cheers and claps and whistles.

Mayor Abbott marched up to him, her hands full of folders and bags, as usual. "Excellent, Detective. I knew I could count on you. Just excellent."

He smiled. "I have a good feeling that the speed dating event will go on."

She squeezed his arm and hurried off. The woman probably had meetings until midnight.

Two men, the Lotter brothers, both mechanics, came up to him. "Great talk, Ford," Harry Lotter said. "I'll tell you, I got—" he leaned closer to whisper "—dumped the other day, and then I saw her walking into the Italian place with someone, hand in hand, and I wanted to punch his lights out. But I air punched instead in my truck. It helped."

"Air punching works," Ford said with a nod, and the two sauntered off in the direction of the refreshment table.

He didn't have to look to the left to know that Danica was heading in his direction. The slight scent of her intoxicating perfume had preceded her. He turned, his heart giving a little flip at the sight of her.

"I'm just going to come out and say it, Ford."

Uh-oh.

"I really need your help with the matchmaking forms. Pauline just dropped fifty more on me!"

He was so relieved that she wasn't talking about them that he would have done anything she asked. "Where and when?" he asked. "Happy to help."

"Oh, phew, thanks. Your house? Right now? Unless you have plans. Candace and Jasper have taken over the living room for a movie night, and I don't want to interrupt their canoodling, you know?"

"Canoodling? I think I last heard that term from my grandmother about the goats. But yes, right now works fine. Follow me home."

Ten minutes later, lots of hands shaken, good-byes said, pats on the back had, they finally left. There were a few low wolf whistles indicating it had been noticed that Ford and Danica left together. He wanted to announce that they weren't together-together, that dating and romance and love led to nothing but heartache, pain and misery.

But, of course, he couldn't. And he didn't really believe that—not for other people. He hadn't even read more of the diary, and he still felt what he'd read so keenly—like the pages, his mother's despair, had turned into sludge that had formed a hard ball in his chest, in his stomach. How could anyone feel good about love, in any context, after reading that?

"My brother Rex had a baking day with his two-year-old son and made pumpkin cheesecake brownies. Want one? And some coffee?"

Danica smiled as she followed Ford into his kitchen. "Aw, that's incredibly sweet to think of Rex at the counter, toddler standing on a chair, both in aprons, covered in flour." She had a sudden image of Ford doing the same with *their* toddler, Danica snapping photos. Yes, she liked the thought of that. "I definitely have to have some of their baking day results."

She stopped short as she recognized the rectangular metal box on the kitchen table. The diary was in there. The diary that had changed everything. Chills slid up her spine.

Clearly Ford caught her noticing it because he grabbed it, but the latch wasn't on and the contents fell out onto the tile floor—the diary and a ripped-up page.

"Oh, boy," Danica said. "I almost feel afraid of the diary, like it might burst into flames or hex me." Okay, probably not the wisest thing to say. But those chills remained at the sight of it on the floor, the tiny pieces of the torn-up page beside it, its secret—maybe thankfully—gone. Whatever it had said was very likely something Ford did *not* need to know.

"Yup. Every time I pick it up I half expect it to burn my hands," he said. "Diaries are heavy stuff. It's where people write their deepest, darkest truths." He knelt down, and put it and the little pieces of paper back in the box.

"I'm sorry about it," she said. "That something meant as a gift is bringing you so much unhappiness."

He stared at her. "A gift? That's not what my father meant it to be."

"He bequeathed it to you for a reason, though. Certainly not to hurt you."

He seemed to be taking that in, thinking about it. He went to the coffeemaker and got busy on that, then opened a container on the counter and put two of the brownies on plates. "I don't know what his intention was. There was no letter with the map. Just the map. Maybe he meant it more as a gesture of goodwill to my mother and wanted me to know that. That he wished he could have returned it to her."

Danica really had no idea. "That is possible. Then maybe you're *not* meant to read it, Ford. Maybe he just wanted you to have possession of it, for your mother, like you just said."

The coffee was ready, so he got out the mugs and poured, adding cream and sugar to hers just as she liked it. He gestured to the table and they sat down, coffee and a brownie in front of each.

He reached into the box and took out the diary, stared at the front and then handed it to her. "Open any page, any random page, and read it. You'll see why the little I read affected me so much—and so badly."

"I don't think I should—"

"Just so you understand, Danica. It's important to me that you do." He put the diary down beside her plate.

"Why?" she asked, her heart hammering.

"Because I feel like you offered me something beautiful, something of yourself, and I let you down. I hate that."

"I didn't ask you to be the father of my child, Ford," she snapped. "I just asked you out on a date."

He lifted up his hands. "Whoa, I know. I just mean…" He stopped and picked up his mug, wrapping his fingers around it.

"I know what you mean. Sorry." She took a quick sip of her coffee and picked up the diary. She'd seen this type of journal so many times in the drugstore and in the bookstore and gift shop in Prairie City. She let out an inward sigh and flipped through, letting her thumb catch on a page. This was toward the end. Probably not the best place to land. "You sure?" she asked him.

He nodded.

She opened the diary a little wider. *Bo has cheated on me countless times. And every time I say I'm going to leave but I never do. Every time I don't, my self-esteem withers. One day, I won't have any regard for myself and I'll just stay, like I don't deserve better. Like Ford doesn't. And he deserves the world.*

Danica's eyes filled with tears, and she put the diary back on the table. "Oh, God."

He nodded. "That's my mother. My *mom*." He was staring at his coffee, looking as down as she clearly was. Danica stood up and went behind his chair, wrapping her arms around his shoulders, her head against his. She felt him take her hands in his, and then he stood up, too, suddenly facing her.

Again he took her face in both his hands and kissed her. She slid her arms around his neck, kissing him back, leaning into him, needing to get closer. When he tightened his arms around her, she felt herself sag. She'd needed this.

"What am I doing?" he whispered. "I'm trying to explain why I can't get involved with you. How'd we end up like this?"

"Because we have strong feelings for each other, Ford," she said, looking right into his eyes, her arms still around his neck. "And there's no denying that or trying to ignore it."

He closed his eyes for a second and took a half step back so that she had to let go of him. Dammit.

"Half the people in that folder you brought over?" he said, gesturing at the matchmaking requests on the table. "They're going to end up crying and heartbroken and divorced. Just like Ellen Dawson."

"So everyone should just give up? Be cynical about the most beautiful thing there is?"

He moved to the counter, leaning against it. "I just know that since I read what little of the diary I did, everything I thought I wanted changed. I now want nothing to do with dating—let alone marriage and kids. I took down the tire swing in the yard, by the way."

She gasped. "You did not."

"I did. The past few days, I'd drive past it out the driveway and it would make me feel like hell."

"Oh, Ford."

He sat back down and took a long slug of his coffee, leaning back and staring up at the ceiling.

"What do you think was on the page your dad ripped up into tiny pieces?" she asked. "What could it have said?"

"I can't even imagine. Not sure I want to. Had to have been bad. It was the whole reason he buried the thing. I thought about asking her friend just so there'd be no loose ends, but that seems like a bad idea. Like I just said, I'm not sure I want to know."

"What friend?"

"A woman named Junie. She and my mom were close when she was married to my dad. When I first got the envelope with the map, I went to talk to her, and she wouldn't tell me anything and made some excuse to get me to leave."

Danica's eyes widened. "Junie? Junie May-wood?"

"You know her?"

"She's family. Estranged family, but family. My mother's cousin. They stopped talking decades ago. I only met her once, at my grandmother's funeral when I was little."

"See? What the hell is the point? Estrangements. Decades without speaking. First cousins?" He shook his head and drained his coffee mug.

"I won't let it rule my life anymore, Ford. The cold front that runs in my family, the grudge holding, the ability to turn away from close relatives. I'm done with it. I wasn't happy in the slightest when my aunt Trudy decided to elope. In the past, I might have let that bother me, thinking that it means she didn't want me or Candace at her wedding. It doesn't mean that at all. It means she wants to elope. My job is to be happy for her. To support her."

"I know how far you've come, Danica. But I feel how I feel."

This was so frustrating. She understood what he was saying. She understood him. She just wished she could help somehow. And not just so they could finally be together, see if this chemistry, their feelings for each other, were solid. She wanted to help him for *his* sake.

"Well, let me just say this. If you want the ultimate closure on this and want to know what that diary page said—" she pointed at the tackle box "—I will drive us over to my mother's cousin's house and ask her, in the name of family, to tell you. Your dad wanted you to have this book. We can't know exactly why. But I know it wasn't to hurt you. I believe that."

He dropped his head back. "I don't know anything, Danica."

She gave him a gentle smile. "I think we'd better eat this amazing brownie. So you can tell that adorable nephew of yours how good his baking skills are, and then we'll jump into the matchmaking forms—if you're still up for helping with that."

"Absolutely," he said. He glanced at his watch. "No calls from Dispatch yet alerting me to crimes of vengeance. That's a good sign."

His smile lit up his face, and she was so happy to see it she almost hugged him. But she didn't.

She could see his shoulders finally relax, along with a muscle in his neck. They started talking about the speech he'd given at the town hall, and he actually laughed a time or two, and so did she. Right now, she had to let all this personal stuff go and give him some space. He was going to need some time.

Either he'd come for her or he wouldn't, and she'd have to accept the possibility that he'd never be hers. Heartbreaking as that sounded.

Danica couldn't sleep. She glanced at her phone on her bedside table—1:28 a.m. She'd already checked on Brandy, hoping the baby might need a little soothing, but her niece was fast asleep. Candace was, too. She'd had a great night with Jasper; apparently they were now officially exclusive and a couple. Her sister had been beaming when she'd told her about their conversation.

And everything was conspiring to keep Danica awake. Wanting what her sister had. Wanting Ford to revert back to wanting six kids. Not that she did, but *that* Ford, who'd dreamed of a house full of children. Wanting him to be at peace with his past and with himself.

She got out of bed, stuffed her feet in her fleecy slippers, and was about to head downstairs to make some herbal tea when she turned right for the door that led to the attic. Her mother had given her two trunks when her parents retired to Arizona, saying that it was full of old stuff of hers and her sister's, and if Danica didn't want it she'd just hurl the trunks into the Dumpster they'd rented to get rid of stuff. Danica had never been very sentimental or pulled by nostalgia, but she liked the idea of there being childhood trunks in the first place. Who knew what was in there, what her mother had kept and why. The idea that Judith Dunbar had kept anything had been a nice surprise, and it had led to Danica feeling more warmly toward her mother when they drove off for their retirement community. Danica's father was a passive, quiet man who'd always deferred to his wife, so her mother loomed larger in her mind when she thought of her upbringing.

She walked up the steep steps into the big space. Not much up here. Seasonal stuff and boxes of Christmas decorations were along one wall. Another area contained Molly's stuff since Molly's house was small and didn't have an attic. Molly was a sentimental saver—there were old posters she couldn't bear to toss and her childhood desk, white with purple knobs on the drawer. Molly was saving it for Lucy.

Danica knelt in front of a trunk and opened it. Her prom dress, wrapped in plastic, greeted her. Danica stared at the slinky black dress she'd been so proud of, had felt so elegant in. There were accordion folders marked Elementary School,

Middle School, and High School. Danica peered through the high school one, full of clippings from the Bear Ridge Buffaloes Student Newspaper. Danica, cheer team co-captain. Voted Best Looking each year. Danica and Troy, Class Couple, also each year. Prom Queen and Prom King. She had photos in her albums in her bookcase and she hadn't looked at them in a while, but the thought of them had long stopped hurting. Time and self-awareness and a little—a lot—of soul-searching did wonders.

In the elementary school file she found what she was looking for. A black-and-white composition notebook with Danica's Dreams written in pink marker in the little box on the front.

She sat down at Molly's desk and opened the book. It was in diary format, each page dated, the first entry in early September, the eve of the first day of second grade. Apparently Danica wrote faithfully every Sunday night at seven-thirty. The book started with how she hoped she'd make a best friend this year and how girls seemed to like her and include her, but she didn't have a best friend like Zoe Parker or Evie Ramez did. The next entry was all about Molly, and Danica grinned as she read about how she'd been paired with Molly in "science lab" where they discovered what happened when you dropped a penny into a beaker full of water. As she flipped the pages, Danica was touched by the sweet, hopeful, curious girl she'd been, happy that she'd found her best friend, a love of the color yellow and wearing pretty clothes, which her mother had been only too happy to indulge her in because she liked her daughters to look elegant.

And then there it was. *May 18. Candace asked me how many kids I want, two like Mommy and Daddy or more or none. I want eight kids. Four girls and four boys. I'll name them all after Molly because she's so awesome. Madeline, Melody, Mia, and Maisy for girls. The boys I'll name Matthew, Michael, Max, and Mason.*

I want to have a huge family. Interesting. She closed the notebook and hugged it to her chest. She definitely couldn't imagine having eight kids. Six kids. Even four. One sounded just right now. But Danica had loved having a sister and she knew she'd want to give her child a sibling. So two.

She stood up and closed her eyes, hardly able to believe how much she'd changed in such little time. She'd broken through her own walls. Ford had done it, too, and he could do it again.

"Dani, you up there?"

Candace.

"I'm coming down," she called.

She put away the notebook and climbed down, turning off the light at the bottom of the stairs.

Candace stood peering at her, looking sleepy. "Brandy was crying, so I helped her work out a little gas, got her back to bed, and then realized the attic door was open and a light was on. What were you doing?"

"I was looking for that notebook you told me about—the one I wrote in about wanting eight kids. You were right."

Candace smiled. "Ha, I knew I wasn't making it up. Mom saved that notebook? That's unexpected."

"Right? Maybe there's more to Judith Dunbar than we both ever realized."

"I think there's more to everyone than most people realize," Candace said. "That's something that's really opened my eyes lately."

Danica nodded. She closed the attic door, hugged her sister good-night, and was pretty sure she'd manage to sleep well tonight after all.

Chapter Twelve

Ford had Friday off, but he'd asked the chief to alert him to any crimes of vengeance. Overnight Thursday: zero. He felt damned good about that. And he'd needed good news. He made coffee and stood at his kitchen counter chomping on a bagel and cream cheese, wishing Danica was still sitting at his table. What he'd give to feel her behind him, her arms around his neck, her perfume enveloping him.

And that kiss. He'd thought about that incredible kiss until he'd finally fallen asleep.

His phone buzzed with a text. His brother Zeke.

Hey, I happen to be on your porch. I got news, bro.

Ford walked over to the door and opened it. Zeke stood there in a brown leather jacket and jeans, a wool hat against April's morning chill. "Why not just ring the bell?"

Zeke peered behind him. "Do I know what you're doing? Or who might be over? I don't want to interrupt anything."

"All alone," Ford said. Not liking how that sounded. "So what's the news?"

Zeke came in and shut the door behind him. "Guess what you are?"

"A detective. Thirty-five. Blue eyed. A great guy."

"Not even warm."

Ford raised an eyebrow. "Your favorite brother?"

"One of them," Zeke said, folding his arms across his chest. "Okay, I'll tell you. Invited to a wedding. Tomorrow night at the lodge."

"Sorry, I have plans," Ford said, then grinned and pulled his brother in a hug. "Congratulations. That's some advance notice."

"The ballrooms have been booked for months, but then there was a cancellation—Cole and Trudy ended up eloping. Molly tried to snag it but even with the family in at the Dawson Family Guest Ranch, she was like five minutes too late and someone had already grabbed it. But then *that* person canceled—apparently an ex came back into the picture. So if we want to marry right here in that perfect room with the deck and view of Clover Mountain, we're saying 'I do' tomorrow. I would have group texted, but Molly said no way. I think she's at your friend Danica's right now."

Even the sound of her name made his heart give a little jump. Which his brother must have picked up on.

"So what's going on with you two?" Zeke asked, sitting on the arm of the sofa.

"We're friends. Bad timing. Once again."

"Oh?" he said, then added, "Oh…yeah, I know about that. And not because Molly tells me anything. Because back in February, when I couldn't decide between buying a house like you did or building on the ranch property, I met with Danica at her office and she told me herself that she wasn't sure she wanted kids. We just got to talking."

February seemed forever ago. Zeke had moved back to town from years away in Cheyenne, having gotten as far as he could from home the moment after high school ended, only to be drawn back because Danica Dunbar had gotten divorced. He'd had a wild crush on her in middle school and thought he'd finally have his chance—only to discover that not only had his long-standing crush not grown up with him, but he was madly in love with Danica's best friend, Molly, Zeke's administrative assistant.

"So Danica doesn't know about kids," Zeke said, "and you want eighteen kids or some crazy number."

Ford dropped down on the sofa, head back against the cushions. "Past tense. Wanted. And six. Like us. But that's done with."

"What's done with? Wanting children?"

Ford sighed. "Yeah. I've been reading my mother's diary and it cured me of all that."

He hadn't planned to read any more of it, but last night, when he'd been unable to think of anything but that kiss and of being in bed with Danica that one and only time, he'd grabbed the diary to reinforce his belief that he was meant to be on his own, the lone wolf he'd always been. No one got crushed that way. He'd read about ten entries, anger and tears warring, and one entry had made him literally sick to his stomach. He'd closed the diary after that and stuffed it in a drawer, done with it. Done with it all.

"Bo broke her heart over and over and was responsible for all her misery," Ford said. "She was trying to take care of their young kid—me—while he was drunk all over town, flirting and humiliating her, drinking and gambling away their income so that she had to get a part-time job in addition to her ranch duties. She'd had to learn some jobs on the ranch she had no idea how to do because the cowboys had left—they weren't getting paid— and it was down to the two of them. One day—I was five—my mother got kicked in the ribs by a wild horse Bo had brought in. She had to go to the clinic because she was in terrible pain. She told me she slipped and fell and cracked one of her ribs but she'd be okay. She didn't want me to blame my dad for a drunken move like trading one of our last goats for that horse. *She* didn't want to blame him. She had to call her friend to pick her up, take her to the clinic and sit with me in the waiting room because Bo had been sleeping off a bender."

Zeke shook his head. "Damn. Sorry you're dealing with this. Why the hell did Dad leave you that damned map in the first place? Why would he want you to find the diary and know all this? What was the point?"

Ford shrugged. "I can't figure that out."

It really made no sense. His dad was negligent and a disaster as a parent, but he'd been loving in his own way to his children. He wouldn't *try* to hurt Ford. He'd left him the map because he wanted him to find the diary and understand something. But what?

His mother's friend would know. Not necessarily what drove Bo to leave Ford the diary but what had been on the page his father had torn up into tiny pieces. Something so terrible it warranted his running out of the house with the diary and burying it just beyond the gate. Weeks later, his mother had left with Ford and their suitcases.

Maybe he'd take up Danica on her offer to connect with Junie, his mom's friend—the same one she'd called for help when the horse had kicked her. Her mom's cousin. But the woman hadn't wanted to talk about her old friend a year and a half ago when he first got the map, and Ford didn't expect her to be any more forthcoming now. He wasn't even sure involving Danica's aunt would help, given that she'd been estranged from Danica's mother for decades.

He looked at his brother, whose eyes reflected his concern for Ford, and he appreciated that. *Family* could be a loaded word, but he could count on his siblings and knew it without a moment's hesitation.

"Let's change this cruddy subject to a better one," Ford said. "Your wedding. I'll be there, of course."

"Yeah, you will. Because you're my best man."

Ford's mouth almost dropped open.

"That's what you get for being the oldest and the one we all went to with everything growing up. If it wasn't for you, things would have been much worse for us, Ford. And that's the truth. You weren't much older, but you were standing between us and Dad."

"That means a lot," Ford said. "I'm honored, Zeke. Thanks for asking me."

Zeke nodded and clapped Ford on the shoulder. "We're having a quick rehearsal in the morning. Meet at the lodge at nine. Come hungry—we're having bagels and coffee. I'll even get cinnamon raisin, your favorite."

"I'll be there."

As Zeke left, Ford realized that after tomorrow he'd be the last single Dawson.

Danica was doing her pre-work yoga video when the doorbell rang. Mayor Abbott with even more matchmaking forms? Ford to say he couldn't live another day without her?

She pulled open the door. It was neither of those two. Molly stood on the porch—and not dressed for work in her usual trademark pantsuit and little scarf. Molly had on jeans, boots and a heavy sweater, her wildly crazy curly brown hair loose past her shoulders. She also didn't have her fourteen-month-old daughter with her.

And she was absolutely beaming. Something was definitely up.

"So," Molly began, her eyes all lit up. "Turns out there was a cancellation at the Dawson ranch lodge ballroom for tomorrow night, and Zeke and I grabbed it. We're getting married tomorrow!"

Danica screamed and wrapped her arms around Molly. They both jumped up and down. "How exciting! What do you need? Everything? I'm supposed to work today, but I can call in and we can head to Prairie City and—"

"I don't need a thing, crazy enough. You know how I always said I wanted to wear my grandmother's wedding gown, which my mother also wore? We had it altered right after Zeke proposed so it's all set. Veil, too. And my grandmother surprised me with the most gorgeous satin heels—not too high, of course. I have 'something old'—my aunt Catherine's diamond stud earrings. 'Something new'—the shoes. 'Something borrowed'—the dress. And something blue is where you come in."

"Ooh, what?"

"Remember the necklace you gave me for my

Sweet Sixteen, the delicate gold chain with the three little sapphire stones in the shape of a heart? I'm wearing that. Gotta represent my bestie."

Danica's eyes misted. "I'm so happy for you, Molly."

"I don't need to ask you if you happen to have a maid of honor gown in that closet of yours. You probably have twenty perfect dresses."

Molly had asked Danica to be her maid of honor the day after she'd gotten engaged. Danica couldn't wait to stand up for her friend.

"Any color scheme?" Danica asked.

"Nope. Any color you want. We're keeping the wedding party tiny. Just the maid of honor and best man."

"Who's doing the honors for Zeke?" Danica asked.

"He's asking Ford as we speak."

Danica swallowed. And of course Molly noticed the gulp and whatever weird thing had happened in her expression.

Her best friend narrowed her eyes. "Exactly what is going on with you two?"

"Absolutely nothing, unfortunately," Danica said. "Well, maybe a little something. But Ford's dealing with some stuff. I really hope we get our chance."

"Hey, if Zeke and I worked things out, you and Ford will, too. It takes the Dawson brothers a while to realize they're actually in charge of their own destiny. But they've had a lot to grapple with. Ford'll come around. I know it, Danica."

"From your mouth…" she said with a nod.

"I'd better get going. My mom's at the coffee shop with Lucy and my aunts and grandmother. We'll be heading over to the ballroom to meet Daisy Dawson and make sure everything's set for tomorrow night. Oh—and rehearsal tomorrow morning at nine—there will be bagels and coffee. Does that work? Sorry for the last-minute notice."

"It works fine. I'll see you then. And congrats again, Molly." She gave her bestie a fierce hug.

And as she watched Molly head to her car from the porch, she was very aware of how badly she wanted to be in her friend's satin shoes, marrying a Dawson brother.

Danica was deciding between two dresses for Molly's wedding—pale yellow halter gown or a very pretty mauve with delicate beading at the waist—when Candace came in, a shopping bag in one hand, baby Brandy in the other. Candace had spent the day in Prairie City with her baby girl, attending a "music for babies" class at the library and window shopping. Her sister put down the bag and dropped into the easy chair between the window and the closet, not looking particularly happy.

"Hey, you okay?" Danica asked, giving her niece's baby curls a little caress.

Candace bit her lip and rested her head atop Brandy's. "I'm fine. Just a little zonked."

Her sister wasn't fine, but she wasn't up for saying why yet.

"What's in the bag?" Danica asked. "Ooh, from Best Dressed?" she added, noting the label.

"Oh, yeah. I was ogling a really pretty dress in the window of that shop when Molly texted me and invited me and a plus-one to her wedding tomorrow night. How sweet was that of her to invite me? I do feel like we all grew up together so I was really touched by her text. I've been trying to conserve money till I get a job, but I had to get the dress in the window for the wedding. It's the prettiest shade of periwinkle."

So why did Candace look like she might burst into tears?

"But now I don't even know if Jasper will be attending the wedding with me. We got into a really bad argument. He might not be the one, after all." Her eyes welled with tears.

Danica sat on the bed. "Honey, what happened?"

"Well, I called him about the wedding and he was excited to go—until I mentioned that I would be bringing Brandy, too. He hesitated for way too long and asked why I wouldn't get a babysitter so we could be assured a great time Saturday night. And it made me really focus on the fact that Jasper hasn't wanted to spend any time with Brandy. Granted, she's five months old and not the most interactive, but she's my child. He's always like, 'Oh, I made reservations for tonight at the steakhouse, your sister can babysit till at least one in the morning so we can go out after, right?' He never suggests the three of us spending time together. In fact, the only reason he agreed to have a movie night here the other day was because we'd had a long day hiking and Brandy was already asleep when I suggested he come over."

"Have you talked about why he's reluctant?" Danica asked.

"He just said we've only been seeing each other for a couple weeks and he wants to get to know *me* first, get to know *us* first as a couple before we get more family oriented. I don't know, Danica. It didn't sit right with me. I told him that since babies were not only welcome but encouraged at the wedding, because Molly has a baby of her own who'll be there, that Brandy would be my plus-one and that he could join us or not. He got quiet after that."

"But he's going, right?" Danica asked, not liking how it this was sounding.

"He said he'd really have to think about it." She held Brandy tight against her, rubbing her little back. "Why didn't I see this before? How could I let myself fall crazy in love with a man who isn't interested in spending time with my daughter? Brandy comes first. That's how it is."

Danica was so impressed by her sister. They hadn't been raised to put children first. "Your priorities are definitely in the right place, Candace. And given how he obviously feels about you, I'm sure he just has to get comfortable with the idea of how serious he's getting with a single mother. Maybe that hadn't hit home for him until now."

"What if now that it has, he walks away?"

"I can't see that happening, but if he does do that, then he's just not your guy. But I think you have to give him a little time. God knows I'm trying to do that with Ford, to not necessarily take him at his word because even though it's important to believe what someone tells you, sometimes they need to do some thinking or soul-searching and come to some new conclusions."

"I hope so. For you and me." Brandy let out a yawn and a little shriek. "Let me go get her to bed and I'll show you the dress."

Danica gave her sister an encouraging smile, her heart pinging as Candace left her room. She'd send up a little prayer tonight for both of them that their fervent wishes would come true. But Danica wasn't so sure that either of them was going to get the happily-ever-after they were hoping for.

Chapter Thirteen

On Saturday morning, Ford poured himself a cup of coffee from the buffet table in the lodge's small ballroom. In attendance at this rehearsal breakfast were the minister, the bride and groom, the bride's parents, her dad—who was giving everyone a gift certificate for two free tacos from his taco truck, Tim's Tasty Tacos in Prairie City—and Danica and Ford, maid of honor and best man. Molly, her mother and Zeke were making last-minute adjustments to the seating arrangements for tonight. Danica and Ford would be seated at the head table, beside each other, and both would give a short speech.

Ford was going to need a little help with that speech. He wasn't feeling particularly solid on everlasting love. Maybe he could find out what Danica had in store for her speech and go from there.

"We keep getting paired," Danica said as she came to the table and poured herself a mug of coffee.

Ford nodded. "It's like the universe is trying to tell us something."

"It definitely is," she said. "Of course, I might be taken by the time you come around."

She was both kidding and not kidding. He could see the glint of humor in her eyes and also the steely resolve.

He wanted to say that he couldn't see coming around, not with the sludge-like gunk in his chest, in his gut, covering his heart. But as he looked at his beautiful Danica, he wanted to have the faith in himself that she did in him, the faith she'd had in herself.

"I guess I'll just have to dance with Brandy tonight," he quipped.

She smiled. "Well, Brandy will definitely be in attendance. Candace's plus-one, we're not so sure about." She explained what was going on.

"Well, he's not wrong," Ford said. "He should get to know Candace better before getting emotionally involved with her baby. They haven't been dating that long."

"She's a package deal, though. There's no Candace without Brandy when it comes to a man in her life."

Ford downed the rest of his coffee. "Nothing wrong with taking it slow, though."

"It's not about slow or fast. It's about accepting that she's a single mother. If he doesn't want to spend time with the two of them, then maybe he's not the guy for her."

"So he has to be all in right away?"

"I didn't say that. But he should be—"

"Boy, do you two bicker like an old married couple," Molly's mother said, pulling Danica into a hug. "I am getting an invitation to your wedding, I hope."

Ford hoped his cheeks weren't as red as Danica's at the moment. She introduced him to Molly's mother, Abby, then her father, Tim, who he talked tacos with to change the conversation. All the conversations. Ford had met Molly's parents at the engagement party Daisy had thrown a couple months ago, but there had been so many Dawsons there that he was sure Abby and Tim couldn't remember who was who.

Luckily the minister called them up to go over

the ceremony, and Danica gave him a lift of her chin and a turn of her heel.

At the altar, he stood beside his brother, and Danica stood beside Molly as the minister went over the vows. He tried not to look at Danica as the words *love, honor, and cherish* were spoken. But as he heard the words *your bride*, he looked straight at her and knew in his heart that she was his bride, that she was the one, that she'd always be. Danica, on the other hand, seemed to be working hard not to catch his gaze. She kept her eyes on the minister or the floor or the red carpet created as an aisle.

Then it was over, Molly's mother talking a mile a minute about adding more flowers. Danica's phone pinged and he watched her read her text, then kiss everyone but him goodbye and hurry out. He wondered what that was about. Since she probably wasn't talking to him, he likely wouldn't find out.

"You like tummy time," Danica cooed to her niece, who was on her belly on a mat on the rug in Danica's living room.

At the end of the rehearsal breakfast, Candace had texted that Jasper wanted to talk and asked if Danica could babysit for a couple hours. This was one time when the two of them would need to really listen to each other, and Danica was happy to watch Brandy.

Besides, she needed a distraction from her thoughts. Danica had started it—getting all quippy with Ford about the universe throwing them together, which did seem very true—and suddenly there had been some uneasy tension in the air between them. Usually they were on the same page about not being on the same page. But this morning she felt only the discord and she hadn't liked it.

And then she'd felt Ford's eyes on her while the minister had gone over the vows. Danica's heart had felt so bruised and poked. She yearned to say those vows, to hear those vows spoken by her own groom, the man she loved.

And the man she loved was Ford Dawson.

"Why is everything so upside down with me and Ford?" she asked the baby, who turned her little head to look at Danica with a big smile, her tiny hands batting at the mat and rug. Danica was sitting beside her, in lotus position, which had taken her months to achieve.

Wait a minute. Danica leaned forward, her heart thumping. What was that in Brandy's hand? Something shiny and silver. A coin? She couldn't be sure.

Danica gasped and lunged for the baby and whatever she'd grabbed, but Brandy brought her hand to her mouth and suddenly the shiny silver object was gone.

A cold sweat broke out across Danica's neck, and she looked all over the rug around Brandy for the shiny silver thing—a dime? She didn't see anything. Oh, God, had the baby swallowed it?

She scooped up the baby and raced out to her car, buckling Brandy into her rear-facing car seat, her hand on the phone to call 911 if Brandy started choking and turning blue, which she didn't. Was it possible she'd swallowed the dime?

Her heart racing, Danica kept one eye on Brandy as she texted her sister, then Ford. Why she'd alerted him, she wasn't sure, but he was the law, and she was in trouble. Scared trouble. She drove to the Bear Ridge Clinic at the tail end of Main Street, a complete mess of tears and fear.

She explained what she was afraid had happened, and the nurse was just finishing asking if Danica was the baby's mother when Candace rushed in with Jasper.

Candace was freaking out, and the nurse took her and the baby into an exam room, shouting out that an X-ray was needed for a five-month-old baby.

Jasper looked slightly green. Danica sat beside him, neither of them speaking, both staring straight ahead at the pale gray clinic walls, the usual signs posted.

"Everything's okay, right?" Jasper asked.

"I think if Brandy wasn't choking or blue or purple, then she's probably okay. She might have swallowed whatever it was I saw in her hand, but it doesn't seem to have lodged in her airway."

"Okay, phew," he said. He stood up. "I should probably go, then."

"Or you can stay," Danica said gently. "I'm sure Candace will appreciate that you're here, that you care," she added, trying not to emphasize the word.

He bit his lip and sat down, then stood up. "I really should go. I'm supposed to be at work. Will you ask Candace to call me when she knows something?"

Oh, Jasper. Wrong move.

"They'll probably be out in fifteen minutes or so, once the X-ray is taken and the doctors read it. Are you sure you can't wait?"

More lip biting. A bit of pacing. "I really need to get to the ranch. You'll ask Candace to call me. I mean, I'll text her, too."

"I'll tell her," Danica said.

He nodded and rushed out. A few seconds later, Ford came hurrying in.

Danica jumped and threw herself into his arms, sobbing. He wrapped his arms around her, holding her close.

"Is she okay?"

"She seems okay," Danica managed between sobs. "She's being x-rayed."

He nodded. "Let's sit down before your legs give out. If she wasn't choking, her airway must be clear."

Danica breathed out. "I think so, too. I hope so. I'm so scared, Ford. I'm such a neatnik—how would a dime get on my rug anyway?"

"Are you sure it was a dime? Maybe just a bit of silver from the play mat that became dislodged or something?"

"I just don't know. It happened so fast. I saw something shiny and silver in her hand and then in a second her hand was against her mouth and the silver thing was gone."

"You did the right thing rushing her here." He had his arm around her, and if he even attempted to move it she'd grab it right back. That arm was keeping her going right now.

"Thank you for coming, Ford. I've never needed anyone more."

"I'm here," he whispered, and tightened his arm around her. She leaned her head against his arm and let out another breath.

Time ticked by so slowly. A few people came in, someone left, and every time there was movement, Danica practically jumped.

Finally, around a half hour later, Candace came into the waiting room with Brandy, holding a rattle in the shape of an elephant, in her arms. Her sister seemed relieved—a good sign.

"She's okay!" Candace shouted. "There was nothing in her esophagus or stomach. Whatever it was you saw, she must have dropped it and not eaten it."

"I'm so sorry I worried you," Danica said, shaking her head. She could not feel more awful.

"No, I'm glad you rushed Brandy here." Candace glanced around. "Where's Jasper? Restroom?"

"Actually he left about a half hour ago. He asked me to tell you to call him when you knew something. He said he had to get to work at the ranch."

Candace's face fell. "Oh." She shook her head, then lifted her chin. "I'd better get Brandy home. She seems tired and the X-ray freaked me out to the point that *I* need a nap."

Ugh. Danica had tried with Jasper, she really

had, but he wouldn't have it. And that really was a bad sign. Or maybe she was being too hard on him, like Ford seemed to indicate she was? She wasn't sure. He shouldn't have left. That much Danica did know. He should have stayed out of support for Candace, to be there for Candace. Even if he was inwardly freaking about what it meant to be getting serious with a single mother.

They headed out, past Candace, who was settling Brandy in her car seat in the back seat of her car. "See you at home in a few."

Danica nodded and walked with Ford to her own car. He opened the door for her, and she practically collapsed on her seat.

"I know we're on the outs right now, in more ways than one," Ford said, "but would you like to be my plus-one to a wedding tonight? I know for a fact you happen to be going to the same event."

Danica gave him a wobbly smile. "It's a date. Or not." She shook her head. "You know what I mean."

"I do," he said, and then they both did a double take. It was so ridiculous, they both laughed.

Oh, Ford. How I love you, she thought as he closed her car door and put a hand to the window before walking to his SUV.

How am I going to ever let you go?

Chapter Fourteen

The Dawsons cleaned up well, Ford thought, watching his brothers and sister as they entered the ballroom for Zeke and Molly's wedding. His brothers wore dark suits, and Daisy was decked out in a long pale pink gown. Maisey, his brother Rex's wife and the head nanny at the ranch, had hired three of her employees from the lodge's babysitting program to work the wedding so that fussy babies could be quieted in a second and little kids would have supervision while they dashed through and under tables as their parents chatted or danced. The wedding was small, under forty people, and there were babies and kids everywhere.

And couples. Even Andrew Morton, the rancher who Ford had been keeping an eye on before and since his talk on the vengeance crimes, was with a date. Apparently, Andrew and Zeke and Molly and Danica had gone to high school together. Ford counted at least three couples that he and Danica had put together. There hadn't been a single crime of vengeance committed since his talk, and if this continued through the weekend, Mayor Abbott would green-light continuing the matchmaking and holding the speed dating event.

Ford stood at the back of the room behind a row of planters with the groom. Zeke's bride was in the small room to their left, getting ready for the ceremony, which was slated to start in about ten minutes. Danica was in there, along with Molly's parents. When he'd picked up his lovely date a bit earlier, he'd gasped at the sight of her. He hadn't seen Danica Dunbar dressed up in a long time; she usually had her hair in buns to avoid it getting yanked by her niece's grabby hands, and very casual clothes that were meant for spit-up and crawling on the floor.

For tonight, Danica wore a long pinkish red gown that skimmed her body, with delicate straps that curved around her shoulders. Her long, silky blond hair was loose down her back, the dress dipping low. How she walked in those at least four-inch heels he had no idea, but she was exceptionally graceful. He couldn't wait to dance with her, an excuse to touch her, hold her.

With their children being watched by a sitter, the Dawson clan came over for hugs and some ribbing, and then the minister gestured to him that it was time for him and Zeke to take their places, so his siblings darted back to their table. The piano player began a classical piece, and a hush came over the room. He and Zeke walked down the red carpet to the front of the room, where an altar had been set up atop three steps. Zeke stood to the side of the minister, Ford beside him.

As maid of honor Danica came walking down the aisle, carrying a bouquet of red flowers, he couldn't take his eyes off her, even as a pint-size outlaw scooted out of his father's arms in the guest chairs and ran up the aisle, his dad quickly catching him. Danica took her place on the other side of the minister, and then everyone turned as the wedding march began. Just past the row of planters he could see Molly's parents and a flash of white, and then they began their procession with Molly being walked down by both Abby and Tim.

He glanced at Danica, who had tears in her eyes, then watched as Molly's parents both lifted her veil and took their seats. The ceremony began, and the minister's words echoed in his head. *Love. Forever. Blessed union.* Ford's tie began to squeeze his neck, and he forced himself not to gnarl a finger in to loosen it. He'd come home to Bear Ridge because he thought he'd changed, thought he was ready for everything the minister was talking about, everything his brother Zeke was about to embark on, and now Ford stood here, that sludge still sitting in his gut, having too much power over him.

And then the bride and groom were kissing to cheers and claps and whistles, and Danica had her arm wrapped around Ford's as they walked back up the aisle together.

"That was such a beautiful ceremony," she whispered. "I tried hard not to cry. My best friend since second grade is now married to the man of her dreams."

"They both looked so happy," he said as they rounded the planters.

The bride and groom were beaming as they joined them behind the planters. The guests were led out onto the huge deck overlooking Clover Mountain, white lights twinkling from overhead as waiters intermingled with trays of champagne.

A waiter came over with a tray, but Zeke and

Molly had started their first dance. Ford and Danica, staring into each other's eyes, took two glasses of champagne each. What was between the bride and groom was so romantic, so intimate, that Ford glanced away, hoping he wouldn't drop his or Zeke's champagne.

"They really do," Danica whispered, her voice full of emotion.

He had that tie-strangling sensation again, but this time it was rivaled by an overpowering urge to take her in his arms and slow dance, too, to look into her eyes and hope to see his future and not the front cover of his mother's diary and the torn-up page, which always quickly replaced any image of possible happiness when it came to thinking about marriage and a life with Danica.

And then the music changed and the guests began coming back in, moving over to their elegant tables. Ford and Danica handed the happy couple their champagne, had a quick toast, and then reached their seats just as the band leader began to announce the bride and the groom.

Ford was sitting between Danica and Molly's dad, who was wiping away tears. The first course was served, a delicious-looking butternut squash soup. The table got busy digging in and sipping their wine.

"Oh my," Danica whispered, peering to the left at Table 4. "Looks like Candace was placed at a singles table."

Ford glanced over. Candace sat chatting with the man beside her, a squirmy two-year-old on his lap. Ford couldn't recall the guy's name, just that he was divorced and an old friend of Zeke's. He'd been in one of Ford's pile of matches and hadn't been easy to pair up. Candace laughed; the guy beaming.

That neck tightening was back. Because this was how it was going to go with Danica and some new guy. She'd be laughing at something funny he'd said, they'd lock eyes and off they'd go into their new happy romance, Ford left standing alone in the cold, like Jasper with Candace. Forever. His decision, right? He was picking this over the woman he couldn't get enough of.

He turned his attention back to his table. Danica was telling Molly's dad that she'd tried one of his special tacos at the food truck he parked in Prairie City and that it was so delicious she got back in line and ordered another. Ford had to agree that Tim's Tasty Tacos were the best in the area. But there was something bigger on his mind than tacos. He knew that when the first course started to be cleared away, he'd be called up, as best man, to give his speech.

The band leader gestured to him, and as he stood, Danica whispered, "I know you'll inspire and touch everyone." Her smile was so genuine that he wanted to pull her into his arms and kiss her.

He went onstage, cleared his throat and kept his gaze on Zeke and Molly. "I'm Zeke's eldest brother, Ford Dawson, so I've known the guy his whole life. Zeke is one of the best people I know. Need a friend at three in the morning—he's there. Need a hand with something hard and annoying when he just got off work—he's there. Need the shirt off his back—it's yours. Zeke came home to Bear Ridge to seek a fresh start in his home-town, and what did he find? The love of his life, a woman he'd known since middle school. Now, Zeke will be a doting and loving father to Molly's baby daughter, Lucy. He'll be a loving, supportive, stand-by-his-woman husband to Molly. I wish all three of them a lifetime of love and happiness."

He handed the mike back to the band leader, cheers and whistles as he left the stage.

Danica passed him on the way up to give her speech as maid of honor, her perfume wrapping around him.

"I've been best friends with Molly since second grade, when we were paired as science lab partners to do an experiment about dropping coins into water. She was my first best friend, and she's been my first throughout my life—the first I share everything with. I've been so lucky to know Molly and have her friendship. An amazing mother, a true friend, a warm bright light to anyone who needs her, Molly is just the best. Zeke, I've heard you say many times the past couple of months that you're the luckiest guy in Wyoming. Yup, you are. And so is Molly. It turns out that she's been waiting for Zeke Dawson since seventh grade—and she's finally got her man. I wish the two of them all the happiness in the world."

More cheers, more claps. Danica barely got to the table before Molly ran over and hugged her tight, then her parents did the same thing.

"Beautiful toast," he said when she sat down beside him.

"Yours, too," he said.

"I love how everything tonight is about promise," she said, smiling at the waiter as he set her petit filet mignon with its side of rosemary roasted potatoes in front of her. "The promise of happiness, of partnership, you know?"

"I believe everything I said about Zeke and Molly. And I believe everything you said."

"That's a very good sign, Ford. You might be very cynical right now, but somewhere, whether on the surface or deep down, you believe love and forever are possible."

"It feels surface. Like it'll all blow away any second. The goodwill, I mean."

"Don't let it," she said.

He turned and looked at her, taking her hand. "Do you think my mother's friend Junie—your mother's cousin—will be more likely to talk to me about my mom if you're there?"

She almost gasped. "I'm so glad you want to talk to her. I think it's the right move. But I have to be honest—I really don't know if I'll have any impact. I haven't seen Junie since I was little. I don't know if I mean anything to her at all. But we should try, Ford. That's what it's about. Trying."

She held his gaze and, dammit, of course she was right, and that was what he was doing. Trying.

"I'll call her in the morning and I'll call you right after," she said. Was it his imagination or had she moved a bit closer to him, her entire demeanor slightly less wary?

He wanted to warn her that *trying* and *accomplishing* were two very different things, but maybe trying was all he needed to do in this case. He had no idea what he'd learn from Junie, if anything, or if it would help or hurt, but if it meant a second chance with Danica Dunbar, he had to try damned hard.

At the moment, seated in Ford's car as he pulled into her driveway after the wedding, all Danica could think about was the good-night kiss that had better be coming. All those hours of romance in the air, toasts about love and permanence, the slow dancing in Ford's arms where she'd melted against him... She wanted much more than a good-night kiss, but she knew they'd have to take things slowly right now.

Just a half hour ago, they'd been wrapped around each other on the dance floor as the band played Etta James's "At Last," and Danica kept thinking, *yes, yes, yes*, her love had come along. She'd been afraid to look at Ford during the romantic, sultry song, thinking it might do him in when he *was* clearly trying, hard, so she just kept her cheek against his, the length of her snuggled up against him. Those moments were absolute heaven.

Candace had left about halfway through; the single dad at her table kept asking her to dance

even though she'd explained she was seeing someone. The guy kept reminding her that her boyfriend wasn't there and that he was, and Candace
had told him that he was a classic mansplainer
and to have a nice life, packed up her baby and
let Danica know she needed to get Brandy to bed.
Danica had walked her out and heard the whole
story of the pushy, smarmy single guy. Her sister
had looked so hurt over what was going on with
Jasper, but when Danica offered to leave with her,
assuring her that Molly would understand, Candace insisted she stay, that she'd go home, put the
baby down and do some moonlit yoga on the back
deck since it was such an unusually warm night
for April in Wyoming, high fifties.

A light was on in Candace's room, and Danica
was glad she was still awake so that they could
talk—and so Danica couldn't get any not-smart
ideas of inviting Ford in. Not yet.

Ford cut the ignition and turned to her, clearly
noticing her peering up at the window. "Is Candace okay?"

"Wish I knew the answer to that, too," she said.
"It's a blow. The first guy she's fallen for and he's
afraid of a fifteen-pound baby with huge blue eyes.
I've never known Brandy not be able to wrap anyone around her grabby little finger."

He smiled. "She is pretty cute. But she's also very real."

"Meaning?" she prompted, not liking the sound of this.

"Meaning that it doesn't make Jasper a bad guy or necessarily wrong for Candace because he's struggling a bit with the fact that she has a baby. It seems natural that he would. He has no experience with babies. He's single. He fell for Candace, and now he needs a little time to get used to the idea of getting serious with a woman who has a child. A very young child."

Ford certainly wasn't wrong about any of that. "He shouldn't have left the clinic, though," she said.

"He's going to get stuff wrong. That's how people grow."

"Answer for everything," she said, sliding a bit of a smile at him.

"It's practically my job."

She laughed, then looked up at Candace's window again, and her smile faded. "She's so hurt. He did leave the clinic when she needed him, needed his support. And instead of coming to the wedding, he told her they needed a little break to both really think about what they wanted."

"I'm not saying it's easy or fun to go through.

But not every relationship is sunshine and roses even in the very beginning. There's a complication between them, and now they're dealing with it. If Candace wants to be with him, she needs to give it some time. If his actions are a deal breaker, then they're not right for each other."

"I guess," she said on a hard sigh. "I do want her life to be sunshine and roses right now. She's come home disappointed in life, in herself. I just want her to be happy."

"Because you're a loving, caring sister. You're the best, Danica."

She grabbed his face and kissed him. And he kissed her back.

"I wanted to do that all night," he said. "You beat me to it."

She smiled and rested her head on his shoulder for a moment, then sat up. "I don't know what's going on with us, if there is an us, if there'll be an us. I just know that we're got something very special."

"Agreed," he said.

"At *least* we're on the same page on that."

He smiled and squeezed her hand.

She squeezed back. "I'll call Junie in the morning, around nine, and I'll call you right after."

He nodded and she got out of the car, leaning

down to blow him a kiss. She hadn't intended to do that, but Ford brought out a spontaneous side of her.

He caught the kiss in his fist and pressed it against his chest in the region of his heart. And that was it, Danica Dunbar was deeply in love.

Chapter Fifteen

Candace had been crying in her room when Danica came upstairs last night, and the two had talked for a good hour. Candace was exhausted, emotionally and physically. She'd broken up with Jasper when she'd gotten home from the wedding, as much as it pained her. She wanted a man in her life who accepted her as a package deal from the get-go, who wanted a baby in his life, who wanted to be her baby's father. She'd told him she needed a man who'd have stayed at the clinic, that it had been a deal breaker. Jasper had been full of "this is all so new, can't we just…" and Candace had felt she had to walk away.

Danica's heart ached for her sister, but this morning Candace seemed stronger and was full of purpose. She and Brandy were dressed and set for a day in Prairie City, where they'd attend a baby event at the library and do some shopping, and tomorrow Candace had two interviews in town at day care centers and was thinking of getting her associate's degree in early childhood education. Danica was so proud of her.

With the house empty and the clock chiming nine, it was time to make The Call, and she was hesitant. She had picked up her phone and put it down on the counter twice already, fortifying herself with a cup of coffee and a bowl of raisin bran. Nine twenty. She knew Ford was counting on her, so she entered June Maywood's name and Bear Ridge in the search engine and up popped her telephone and address. She still lived in the same house she had when Danica had last seen her, about ten minutes away in a more rural stretch of town. No surprise. Junie didn't like close neighbors or trespassers on her property, like in-town dogs or kids waiting for the school bus.

Danica pressed in the number and held her breath, then slowly let it go.

"Who's this?" Junie said by way of hello.

"Junie, this is Danica Dunbar, Judith's daughter," she said, and mentally crossed her fingers that Junie didn't hang up.

"The pretty Realtor with the long blond hair," Junie said.

Huh. Junie had kept tabs on her? That was un-expected. "I've worked at Blue Ridge Realty for ten years now. I definitely found my calling."

"Are you calling because your mother's gone?" Junie asked.

Danica felt herself frown. "No. My parents are alive and well and retired to Arizona. They have several orange trees in their yard." She bit her lip and thought she'd better get to the point. "Junie, I'm calling because someone I care about… Oh, I'm just going to say this outright. The man I'm in love with is looking for some missing pieces of his past. And it turns out you were close to his mother. We're hoping you can shed some light—"

"Are you talking about Ford Dawson?"

"Yes, Ford. He's—"

"I know what he wants to know. He came around about a year and a half ago after that rat bastard father of his died. I'm surprised it took Bo that long to meet his maker."

"Well, you know then that his dad left him a map to where he buried his mother's diary. Ford tried to find it for the past year and a half and had no luck until just recently. He found it buried just beyond the gate of the Dawson Family Guest Ranch."

"Figures. Ellen never thought to look outside the ranch gates. Drove her nuts not to have her diary."

"Will you talk to him, Junie? He read some of the diary and it has him all tied up in knots. It's made him feel like pursuing a family for himself is a bad idea, that it'll only bring despair like it did for his mother."

"Well, he's not wrong. Ellen ended up alone, a single mother. I've been divorced for almost twelve years. But I have dogs so I'm set."

Say you'll talk to him. Say you'll bring him the peace he needs.

"I'll make you a deal, Danica. I don't get around well these days because I have a bad hip. You bring me a cheesecake from the bakery, and I'll talk to Ford."

Danica almost pumped her fist in the air. "You have a deal. What time should we come over? If today works for you?"

"How about noon? If you could also pick me up a sandwich or something, that would be nice."

"Sure thing, Junie. Any particular kind? BLT? Chicken salad?"

"I do love chicken salad on a good rye," June said.

Danica smiled. "Got it. See you then."

Instead of a "see you then" or a goodbye she got a click in the ear, but Danica had a good feeling about this. About Ford getting his information—and a longtime estrangement coming to an end. Junie had a bad hip? Didn't get around easily? Danica could be a help. Her mother's cousin had opened the door, even if just a sliver, and Danica was going to walk right through.

Ford picked up Danica at ten forty-five and now they were en route to Junie Maywood's home, with two cheesecakes—one plain, one raspberry—and a chicken salad sandwich with a side of homemade potato chips from the Bear Ridge Diner, which had won Best Chicken Salad in Converse County for the past five years.

"So this really does sound promising on two levels," Ford said. "If I'm reading her right, she sounds open to talking to me about my mother, and she sounds open to developing a relationship with you—if *you're* open to it, that is."

Not that he wasn't nervous as hell about what Junie would reveal to him and to Danica. For all he knew, his mother had done something god-awful that had led to that torn-up diary page. And maybe Danica's mother had done something god-awful that had led to her and her cousin's estrangement. Something neither he nor Danica would want to know.

"I am. I barely remember her from childhood, but I know she's my mother's first cousin, and if they had a falling-out that lasted decades, that's not about me—it's about them and foolishness. I'll take all the family I can get."

Such was the problem of jumping into the unknown willingly. You never knew what you'd get.

"Speaking of family," he said as he turned onto the service road that led to Junie's house, "how's your sister?" Danica had told him about the breakup with Jasper, and how sad Candace was. Knowing Jasper—though granted, not well beyond the basics—the guy was likely miserable, too. Ford understood where they were both coming from and didn't think either of them was wrong. But that wasn't going to bring them back together, either.

"She's very sad but she's focusing on her future— she has interviews lined up tomorrow and she's thinking of going for her degree in early childhood education. I think she's going to be okay. She just needs some time."

He nodded. "And she's lucky to have such a supportive sister."

"You know, when I was going through my divorce and I didn't have any family support because we just weren't close enough to warrant it—emotionally or distance-wise—I didn't even really lament it because I didn't know otherwise. It never would have occurred to me that my sister might rush to my side or that my aunt Trudy would call every night to check on me. Now, if one of them was hurting, I would do just that. And I think they would for me. So much has changed."

"Good," he said. He knew she had Molly and her friends at the realty, but family brought a special comfort.

"How much farther to Junie's, would you say?" Danica asked, glancing out the window. "I want to mentally brace myself."

"You think she'll be difficult? Withholding?"

"I'm thinking no. Wanting cheesecake and a chicken salad sandwich—she struck a very easy deal to meet with you. I sensed a warmth under the prickly. But we'll see. I've learned not to get my hopes up about anything. Expectations can be easily squashed."

He glanced at her, but she kept her eyes on the windshield. She was talking about him, he figured. And once again, the sludgy feeling that was starting to dislodge wedged back in some. He hated hurting her. But that was what he'd been doing lately.

"Actually, we're here," he said, turning onto Rural Route 22. "Her house should be just down this road, two miles or so."

They were quiet as they approached the small farmhouse on acres of property. The place was a bit run-down. Two dogs, a shepherd mutt and a tiny yapper, came barreling off the porch as Ford pulled into the gravel driveway.

The front door opened and out came Junie Maywood. She was tall and slender, like Danica, with very straight ash-blond hair to her collarbone. She wore jeans and a fisherman's sweater and felt clogs. Ford wasn't sure of her age, but since his mother and Junie had been friends from school, he figured she'd be around fifty-five or so.

"I don't remember her," Danica said. "How sad. My mother's first cousin, who I definitely know I met, and she doesn't look at all familiar."

"Her coloring and features are similar to yours and Candace's," he noted.

"And my mother's."

Junie stood on the porch, arms crossed against her chest.

"Well, here goes everything," Ford said, unbuckling his seat belt.

He got out and held up a hand in greeting, and Junie did, too, a good sign. Danica carried the bags with the cheesecake and the sandwich, glanced at him, and then started toward the porch.

"Oh, wonderful," Junie said with a little clap. "The Bear Ridge Diner has the best chicken salad sandwiches in the entire county."

"I know it," Danica said. "I just love their food." She walked up the porch steps, the dogs at her heels, sniffing the air.

"Good golly, you're pretty. Of course, you were as a little kid. Everyone said you and your sister would grow up to be supermodels."

Danica smiled. "You look so much like my mother."

Junie's face fell, and Ford could tell from Danica's expression that she instantly regretted saying it.

"Your mother was some piece of work," Junie said. "Has she changed at all? Or is she still a cold fish?"

Danica seemed taken aback. "Well, my mother was never very warm and fuzzy, but I don't feel comfortable talking about her that way. She is my mom, no matter what."

Good for you for speaking your mind, he thought. Just as Junie was.

Junie shook her head. "You and your sister were both such respectful little girls even at five, six years old. Guess there's worse things to be."

"Trust me, there are," Ford said. "I'm a cop, remember?"

Junie laughed. "I remember. Well, come in. I'd like to try that sandwich. Like I told Danica, I don't get into town much, so I make my own chicken salad, and it's good, but I love getting takeout."

"Me, too," Ford said. "I pretty much keep the Bear Ridge Diner in business." He glanced at Danica, hoping she didn't mind the rapport he was trying to build with Junie. She'd already slighted Danica's mother, and it was clear that hadn't sat well with Danica.

They went inside. The house was small and cozy. They went into the living room, and Danica set the bags on the coffee table.

Junie poked her head in the bag. "Ooh, you brought me an iced tea. I love iced tea." Junie unpacked and brought over a standing tray, on which she set the container from the diner. "Can I get you two anything?"

Ford could tell she was hoping the answer would be no so that she could drop down in the chair and dig in. "I'm fine, but thank you."

"Ditto," Danica said. "You go ahead and eat. I love the diner's homemade potato chips."

"Scrumptious," Junie said, popping one into her mouth, the dogs sitting patiently by her side, clearly hoping for a crumb or two tossed their way. Junie did not disappoint them.

"Junie, why did you and my mother stop speaking? I wasn't going to ask—I was planning to wait to see if you wanted to bring it up, but I have to know. What happened?"

"Your mother told me I could do better than Jim Peffernel. That's what happened. He dared to be on the short side for a man, for one. And he worked as a ranch hand so she thought he wouldn't amount to much."

"Jim Peffernel?" Ford said. "He owns one of the biggest ranches in town."

Junie nodded. "Yup, he sure proved your mother wrong. It's why he got so successful."

"Wait, what do you mean?"

"Well, my dear cousin Judith was over at my house one day, baking something with her aunt, my mother, and she was telling my mother how awful it would be if I ended up marrying Jim since he'd never earn much and I'd be poor and so would my kids. I remember my mother telling Judith that he was just starting out and everyone began at the bottom, and he was very cute, and Judith said but he's short. My mother just shook her head, but apparently Judith took it upon herself to tell Jim that he was beneath our family and should find a girlfriend more suited to his station."

Danica gasped loudly. "No she did not."

"Oh yes, she did," Junie said, putting down her sandwich. "Because Jim told me so and I confronted her, and I told her I was done with her, and she said fine with her. And we never spoke again. We weren't particularly close before that, kind of competitive with each other, so both of us liked not having to deal with the other. We were in our late teens and since our parents weren't very close, they didn't push the issue."

"What happened between you and Jim Peffernel?" Danica asked.

"Oh, we kept dating for a few months but it fizzled out. He had such a great sense of humor, but we didn't have much in common. We stayed friendly, though. A couple years later, I ran into him and he said he'd never forgotten my cousin's nasty words and that it propelled him to keep striving and that he'd saved up enough to buy his own small ranch. His little empire grew from there."

"Good for him," Ford said.

Danica nodded. "Yeah, good for Jim Peffernel."

"And that's the stupid reason why your mother and I have been estranged for almost thirty years. I had my good friend Ellen Dawson, so I didn't miss Judith much."

"You and my mother were close till the day she passed when I was in the police academy," Ford said, his chest tightening. "I miss her every day."

"Yeah, me, too," Junie said. She took a big bite of her sandwich, then popped another chip into her mouth. "Wow, this is really good. I appreciate you two bringing this over. And the cheesecakes. Boy, am I looking forward to a slice."

Danica smiled. "We brought you two kinds. We couldn't choose between plain and raspberry."

"You're my kind of people," Junie said, then bit into the second half of her sandwich.

Danica glanced at Ford, and he thought she seemed pleased or more settled, perhaps. She'd learned the story behind the estrangement, and it wasn't something that would keep her up at night. Junie didn't strike Ford as particularly easygoing, but he had a feeling Danica would actually enjoy bringing her aunt chicken salad sandwiches and spending time with her.

"So there's the thing," Ford said. "I'm going to be very honest here. I have very strong feelings for Danica. She's an amazing person. But this diary has me all messed up. Entries about my mother sobbing and praying her husband would change his ways. Seeing him kissing other women in alleyways off Main Street in broad daylight. Needing to go grocery shopping but finding his paycheck spent on gambling and liquor." He shook his head. "I moved back to Bear Ridge to start fresh, settle down. Then I read some of the diary and everything inside me seized up and went cold."

Junie nodded and took a sip of her iced tea. "I get it. Your father was a disaster as a husband and father. Good-looking, but a real mess."

"Yeah, he was," Ford agreed.

"But he got one thing right. Somehow he made six terrific kids with three different women. And he tried to save your mother from himself. I told Ellen she should leave your dad over and over, but my words fell on deaf ears. But boy, when she gave up, when she wrote that she'd lost any self-esteem or sense of self that would make her pick herself up and take her son and leave her rat bastard husband, guess what your father did?"

Ford leaned forward, pinpricks breaking out along the nape of his neck. "What?"

"Well, he'd found her diary and was reading it. That's how he knew she was giving up on life, on herself—because it was the final entry. He read that page and freaked out. He tore it out and ripped it to shreds and told her she had to leave him for her own good. She was furious that he'd read the diary and tried to get it out of his hands but he grabbed some old box, shoved in the diary and the torn-up pieces, and ran out of the house with it. She chased after him but lost track of him. He kept telling her to leave him, that she deserved better, but she was so out of steam in every way that she couldn't see it anymore."

"But she did leave," Ford said. "She packed our suitcases and we left."

Junie nodded. "Because one day your father was drunk and she came home from her part-time job, scared as she was to leave you alone with him, and he'd passed out across you so that you couldn't move. When she got him off you, you were all sweaty and practically blue. Your father could have suffocated you, Ford. She packed that day and left."

Ford stood up and went to the windows, tears stinging his eyes. Hell, he wanted to know, hadn't he?

"So your father wanted to save your mother from him, and she finally saved you from him, and that's what happened."

"Junie," Danica said. "Why do you think his

dad left him the map to the diary? Why do you think Bo wanted Ford to read it?"

"To show he cared about Ellen and his little son. That he couldn't bear what he'd read, that his long-suffering wife had given up and was planning to stay with a cheating alcoholic who'd destroyed his family legacy—the Dawson Family Guest Ranch. He wanted her to have better. He loved her, much as he could love anyone, and he wanted her to find happiness, a better life."

Ford dropped his head in his hands, then finally looked up. "Well, I appreciate you telling me. I'm not sure I want to know any of this. It's so damned...sad."

Junie nodded. "Yeah. But it's life. And life isn't a bucket of clams or a chicken salad sandwich from the diner. It's messy."

"Messy is right," Ford said. "But you know this story from my mom. We really can't be sure what Bo thought or intended."

"Can, too," Junie said. "Because Bo Dawson himself came to see me the day after she'd left him. Wanted me to relay that message loud and clear to Ellen next time I saw her and to say he was sorry. And that he loved you, more than either of you would ever know, but he had a problem and he didn't want to deal with it, and leaving him was the right thing."

Suddenly everything was flipped but still felt so heavy. The sludge was less inside him than sitting on his shoulders now. He had a lot to think about.

"Family can be great or full of hardship and sometimes both," Junie added. "It's why I'm happy with my dogs. No arguing. Just unconditional love. They're all I need."

"Well, I'd like us to get closer, Junie," Danica said. "If you want. Besides me, there's my sister, Candace, and her five-month-old baby, Brandy. And our aunt Trudy, our dad's sister. She's in Vegas on her honeymoon right now. I'll bet they'd love for us all to get reacquainted."

"Oh, I remember Trudy," Junie said. "I liked her."

Danica smiled. "Maybe I can bring Candace and Brandy over soon?"

"How about tomorrow?" Junie asked. "I love babies. As long as they don't throw up on me or pee on me."

Danica laughed, and then she glanced at Ford; he could feel her eyes on him, and he moved back over to the window, looking out, the little dog sniffing his foot.

"We'll come over with breakfast," Danica said. "Eight o'clock?"

Junie nodded. "Perfect. I love the bagels at the bakery, particularly sesame. And bacon scallion cream cheese."

"Gotcha," Danica said with a smile. "Well," she added, standing up. "We'd better get going. I'm so glad we connected."

Ford turned. "Thank you, Junie. If it weren't for you, the story would have stayed buried with my parents, and I needed to know, regardless of how awful it is."

"Yup," Junie said. "The truth matters."

They petted the dogs goodbye and left, and Ford wasn't sure who let out the biggest sigh of relief to be back in the car—him or Danica.

"God, that was intense," she said.

"Yeah. Good word for it."

"You all right?" she asked. "That was a lot to take in."

"I don't know, honestly. I feel like hell."

A montage played in his head—leaving the Dawson Family Guest Ranch main house with his mom and their suitcases, visiting his dad on weekends and finding him passed out drunk often, getting a kind new stepmother, Bo getting divorced from his second wife, and Ford being a "father figure" to his not much younger half siblings, Zeke, Rex and Axel…paying for groceries and Christmas and birthday gifts when his dad drank and gambled money, watching him destroy the guest ranch after his grandparents died. The heartbreak of Bo's third wife dying from cancer, leaving two kids, his brother and sister, Noah and Daisy… Bo destroying the guest ranch and himself. And then his father's funeral, the six Dawson kids holding hands, barely able to speak through their complicated grief. The scattering—and then coming back together where they'd all begun. The ranch.

Danica leaned over and put her arms around him. They sat like that in the gravel driveway until Ford said he had to get out of there.

Then he drove into the nature preserve and parked by the river, and he opened his arms and she fell into them. They stayed like that for a good long time, neither of them saying a word.

Chapter Sixteen

After dropping Danica off at her house with promises to check in by text or phone that night, Ford didn't want to go home and be alone with his gloomy thoughts, but he didn't want to talk to anyone, either, even his brothers or sister. His dad was their dad, yes, but he was the lone Dawson who didn't share a mother with any of his siblings. He drove around town for a while, pulling over when he noticed a guy, maybe late thirties, receding hairline, ducking between cars in the diagonal spaces along Main Street. *What are you up to, buddy?* He got out of his SUV and kept a surreptitious eye on the man. Ford glanced up ahead; a young couple—

they looked like high school kids—were walking hand in hand and reading the menus on the doors of Bear Ridge's few restaurants.

Ah. Perhaps a crime of vengeance was about to ruin the run of good behavior among the daters. The young woman couldn't be older than eighteen. *Way too young for you, dirtbag*, Ford thought, watching the skulker dip in along the next car, rush two cars up, and then reach for something in his pocket. Ford was about to call out to distract him from whatever awful thing he was about to do when he saw a small heart-shaped box of chocolates in the guy's hand.

"Psst, psst!" the skulker called out. The guy walking with the young woman looked over and the other man, kneeling down to avoid being seen, gestured him near. "You forgot this. I didn't want to embarrass you by having your date see your old dad chasing after you."

The young guy smiled. "Thanks, Dad." He pocketed the little heart-shaped box and rejoined his date, the dad slipping away.

So this was what he'd come to. Seeing negativity in everything. Not who he wanted to be.

He got back in his car and drove around awhile longer, finding himself on the road to the Dawson Family Guest Ranch. Maybe he just needed to be there, to let everything Junie Maywood had told him earlier gel in his head while he was right where it had happened.

Once he'd arrived at the ranch, he drove up to the main house where the argument had taken place and then turned around, parking by the gate-house and walking over to the creek. He knew the spots the guests wouldn't go; what looked like heavy brush actually hid a winding path that led to the water's edge, where he could just sit and think. Or not think. The sky was lit up with stars, the moon casting its glow over the water. He sat back against a big rock, watching a brown frog hop at the edge of the creek and disappear between the little rocks nestled there.

What was he supposed to do with everything he'd heard? The whole story was nuts. His father had drunk and gambled and cheated the life force out of his young wife, to the point that she'd given up on expecting anything and had been planning to stay with her husband. Said husband read this in her diary and felt so bad that he wanted her to leave him. Great. Ford was supposed to feel better about any of this? The truth Junie had mentioned only made his heart hurt.

His father had been an addict, yes. And some-where in that tall, lanky body of his, he'd loved his first wife and maybe that was how he'd shown it. He had saved Ellen Dawson, perhaps, by driving her out. Hell, maybe he'd collapsed drunk on his five-year-old son on the sofa knowing it would be the last straw, that she'd be home at six and would push him off his little son, then pack and leave.

The only thing Ford knew with absolutely certainty was that he wished Danica was here right now. They'd sat in his car for over a half hour, silent, just taking comfort in each other's company, presence, the shared knowledge of some hard stuff to bear between them. Maybe he needed a good night's sleep and things would be clearer in the morning.

He stood up and walked back through the brush to his vehicle, the car lights on an old Jeep almost blinding him.

"Oh hey, Ford," someone called out the window.

He peered closer, shielding his eyes. Jasper, Candace Dunbar's ex-boyfriend.

"Hi, Jasper. You all right?" he called over as he walked up to the Jeep.

Jasper looked away for a moment, then back at Ford and burst into tears, covering his face with his hands. "No, I'm not okay." He shook his head, swiping under his eyes with the back of his hands. "Oh, God. Am I really crying in front of you?"

"It's okay. Trust me, I know what's it like to be in a different mindset or place than the woman you care about and have it screw up everything. I'm right there, Jasper."

"Yeah? You gonna fix it?" he asked.

Hey, I'll ask the questions here, he thought, his collar feeling tight again. "Let me ask you, Jasper. This thing with you and the fact that Candace has a baby. What is it exactly that scares the hell out of you?"

"I'm scared enough of how I feel about her," he said. "I've never felt this way about anyone and I've had a lot of relationships, mostly short ones. But being a father? I don't know anything about that. I didn't exactly have a role model in that department, let's leave it at that."

"Yeah, me neither," Ford said. Although maybe in his own way, his father had tried. In some twisted way. As June had said, life was messy. "But it sounds like losing Candace is worse than your fears about fatherhood."

"It is. But every time I think about rushing over to see her and tell her I love her and I'll be a good father to Brandy, that I need to develop some actual confidence in that department, I think about how Brandy is just five months old. If I marry Candace, I'll be in that baby's life from the start.

I'll be all she knows as a dad. And what the hell do I know about being a father? I barely know mine. I could screw up, you know?"

"I don't see why you would if you love Candace and care about the baby," Ford pointed out. "I mean it's your feelings that dictate how you act. Your sense of responsibility toward them. If you have both of those things, you're golden."

Jasper brightened considerably. "I never thought of it like that. It's kind of like my mom always telling me if you think you can, you can. She was always trying to get me to believe more in myself."

"She sounds wonderful," Ford said. "And she's right. If you think you can, you can."

How many times had Ford read *The Little Engine That Could* to his two-year-old nephew? Ten times in the last two months? Danny loved that book. Why hadn't such a simple lesson knocked into his head before now?

And why the hell couldn't he apply that to himself? His situation was different from Jasper's, though it didn't sound all that different. Maybe Jasper didn't have a harrowing diary and history and story lurking in his parents' past, but he'd had his own troubles when it came to his father.

"What if I'm too late?" Jasper asked. "She broke up with me."

"Tell her how you feel. Tell her the truth. Kick fear to the curb. Let how you feel about Candace make your decisions for you."

Ah, he thought. That was the difference between him and Jasper. Ford wasn't scared; fear wasn't what was ruling him. No, it was more like horror that had Ford all turned around—upside down.

"I'm going to see her right now," Jasper said. "Thanks, man."

Ford nodded and watched the red taillights until they disappeared. He'd go home, sleep on it all and hope his own words came back to him in the morning. Maybe he'd find some peace for himself.

He pulled out his phone and texted Danica: Drove around, stared at the creek, had an unexpected conversation. Headed home now to try and sleep on everything. If I can.

She texted back right away: I think you need to do something with the diary, Ford. Something ceremonial to let it go, to say goodbye. You know what you know and maybe honoring that, in whatever way feels right, is the way to go. Oh my gosh, Jasper is at the door to see Candace! Crossing my fingers.

He looked up at the stars, glad about that. At least one couple would be reunited tonight.

* * *

Ford sat at his kitchen table with a beer and a slice of the pie his brother Rex had dropped off from another baking day with his toddler. He kept thinking about what Danica had said.

I think you need to do something with the diary, Ford. Something ceremonial to let it go, to say goodbye.

Maybe. But what? He wanted to honor his mother in some way, but also acknowledge what his father had tried to do to roust Ellen Dawson from her terrible rut.

He thought about where his parents had met, at a park in town where his mother used to walk her little dog. Bo had been stood up on a blind date there by a woman who'd heard about his reputation, or so his father had said, and then Ellen's wire terrier had peed right on Bo's pant leg. They'd had a good laugh about it, and Ford always remembered his mother saying that it was either a wonderful way to meet someone or an ominous way that foretold of not great things to come. Life is a mix, she'd always said.

She'd loved Bo Dawson and he'd loved her. There had been some very hard times, but in the end, Ford decided that all he needed to know was that he'd been conceived in love. Not everything worked out. Some things did. Some things you had to fight for. Seemed to him that his mother had fought for her marriage and she'd lost, but she'd tried. In the end, her husband had loved her enough to save her, force her to start fresh. Ellen Dawson had gone back to school, she'd painted in her spare time, and she'd doted on her only child. She'd been so proud of him when he'd joined the police academy; her father had been a police officer.

He smiled as he remembered his mother, her favorite phrases. He was ready to put the diary to rest where it belonged, where the two people who were the star of it had tried in their own way to be together—and then not. Theirs had not been a magical love story blessed by the stars. If his dad had been a different person, he and Ellen Dawson might have been more like Ford's grandparents, married decades, solid. Instead, his father was who he was and had had three wives, breaking their hearts, breaking his kids' hearts. He shook his head, picked up the damned tackle box and headed back out.

A half hour later, he pulled into the Bear Ridge Park, a huge recreation area with trails and picnic tables and footbridges over the creek. He imagined his parents meeting here, the dog peeing on his father's leg, Bo laughing. He would find that very funny.

At the park, Ford found a good spot off the beaten path, where no one would likely notice the disturbed earth; soon enough it would be covered by wind-blown brush and the diary would have a forever resting place. He knelt down and dug a hole, then put the box in, diary and the torn-up page inside, and covered it with the dirt, packing the top layer tightly and adding some leaves and twigs.

There. It was at peace, even if he still wasn't. He'd work on that, try to understand both his parents—or maybe just accept what he'd just been thinking about: that they were who they were and it wasn't his place to judge either of them, especially now that they were gone. Judging would only leave him his own wounds to fester, his memories to be sour.

He pulled out his phone: Meet me at the park? I'm on the footbridge near the wishing well. I want to show you something.

She texted back immediately: Be there in three minutes.

He'd let the diary go. Now he'd let Danica go.

This was it, Danica thought. Ford was finally free and now they could be together. He would put the tire swing back in his front yard. The image of that tire on the big oak filled her mind, her heart leaping, butterflies zipping around in her stomach—in a good way.

If Jasper had surprised and shocked her sister with a change of heart, anything was possible, and Danica knew that Ford had already been there, been ready, until the diary had changed things for him. Maybe he was going to tell her that he was taking her advice to do something ceremonial with the diary and wanted her opinion on what, exactly. She wasn't sure where the park fit in, but it must have some significance.

As she hurried from her car to the bridge where Ford had said to meet him, she thought about all Candace had told her about her talk with Jasper a little while ago. Apparently, he'd come over, expression and voice clogged with emotion, and apologized profusely for blowing it at the clinic and assuring her that would never happen again. How he'd be there for her, through good times and bad, and that he'd step up even if he had no idea what the hell he was doing. He'd figure it out, he'd said, because he was madly in love with her. And he wanted to learn how to be the father he'd never had. He wanted to start tomorrow afternoon, showing Brandy the petting zoo at the Dawson Family Guest Ranch, then hitting up the toy store to buy her something special that she'd have forever.

Turns out he'd had an inspiring talk with Ford when he'd run into him earlier tonight after his shift at the ranch. That had almost made Danica cry. Ford had been throwing around lines from *The Little Engine That Could*? A child's book that he'd clearly read his nieces and nephews. The man was so ready, so there, and unless Danica was reading this all wrong, Ford was going to tell her that he'd taken his own words to heart.

As she arrived at the wishing well, she could see him on the footbridge, looking down at the creek. Her Ford. He turned at the sound of her footsteps.

"My parents met in this park. My mom was walking her dog and it peed on my dad's leg. The most auspicious beginning. That should have clued them in."

A chill slid up Danica's spine. He did not sound remotely at peace.

"Their love story and what it turned into isn't your story, Ford. It's theirs. You came out of that union, but you're your own person. Your father had some good traits and you have those. Your mother had some beautiful traits and you have those. Take the good and let the sadness go with that diary. What did you decide to do with it?"

"That's what I wanted to show you." She followed him to some brush, which he held aside for her to walk through, and there was a small clearing near a cluster of trees. "I buried it here. I put their story to rest. I feel like I returned the diary to my mother, letting her have her truth. My father's truth is also out there now because I know what happened. I let it go, Danica. And that's thanks to you."

"I'm glad to hear it." But... She felt a hard *but* coming, a heartbreaking one. She tried to gear up for it, to brace herself, but she was looking at the man she loved.

"Everything I came back to Bear Ridge for? Settling down, having six kids... That's just not who I am anymore or what I want. I know you were hoping I'd come around, revert back. But I've changed, Danica. And it feels irrevocable."

Tears stung her eyes. "Do you love me?" she asked.

"It's not about that."

"Oh yes, it is. Do you love me?"

"Danica, this is about *me*—not us. I think you just need to accept where I am and find yourself the future you want. It's not with me."

He'd turned away as he'd said that, and she knew it had cost him to say that, that it would bother him, even if that was how he'd felt. Ford wasn't one to shoot arrows in a broken heart. And he just had.

"I'm just trying to be very clear," he said.

"No, Ford. You're not *trying* at all." She turned and ran back to the path, then to her car, wanting to sit and cry but she had to get out of there. The park where she'd left her heart behind.

Chapter Seventeen

In the morning, Danica just wanted to stay in bed, her quilt pulled up to her neck, a box of tissues under the covers with her for easy access. But she was supposed to be at Junie's at eight o'clock—with her sister and the baby, and Candace was excited to meet a long-estranged member of the family whom she barely remembered.

Everything about her family will be different for Brandy, Candace had said last night.

Danica wished Ford could look at it that way. Why couldn't he see that he could be the change? His siblings had done it. Why was he so stubborn about this? She couldn't understand it.

When she'd gotten back from the park last night, Candace was looking at the old photo album she'd found in her trunk. There were pictures of Junie and Judith, and their expressions alone told a story. First cousins who could not stand each other. Danica had told Candace only a little about what happened with Ford, that the timing just wasn't right and she was going to have to move on. Candace had been so touched and moved by the family photo albums, which she hadn't seen since she'd left home at eighteen, that Danica hadn't wanted to inject her misery.

She'd saved bursting into tears for her own bedroom and had slept like hell.

Now she threw off the covers and took a long, hot shower, then had a strong cup of coffee. Her phone pinged, and Danica grabbed it, her heart hoping it would be Ford, but it was Aunt Trudy, sending photos from her honeymoon. Danica called Candace down and they smiled at the pictures, Trudy and Cole looking so happy.

One day, she'd find happiness for herself, once she was good and over Ford Dawson, which was going to take a while. In the meantime, she'd continue bringing couples together in Bear Ridge. Always a matchmaker, never a match.

The family photo album was on the kitchen

table, and Danica took her coffee over and sat down, flipping through it. She stared at photos of her mother, never quite smiling, even in pictures with her husband. Her mother was who she was, but Danica was who she was. And she wasn't someone who ignored or avoided family.

She picked up her phone and pushed the button on her mom's contact page.

"Danica? Something wrong?"

Danica shook her head. "No, nothing at all. I just wanted to say hi and hear your voice. It's been a while."

"Oh, how thoughtful of you. Well, I'm just here with your father, sitting on the patio admiring the orange trees. We're having fresh squeezed orange juice from our own backyard. Isn't that something?"

"Nothing beats it," Danica agreed. They talked about oranges and the weather, and then Danica mentioned that Candace and Brandy had moved back to Bear Ridge and were staying with her. Her mother asked how they were but said nothing about visiting. *People are who they are*, she thought again. *You can't change them just because you want to. They have to want to change.*

Like Ford.

Danica decided not to mention that she'd reconnected with Junie or that she and Candace and the baby were going over for breakfast. That would sit weird in her mother's head, and Danica knew it. She'd save it for another time, maybe. Or maybe she'd just keep it to herself. Judith and Junie were the past, and Danica's relationship with Junie was the future. Her mom said she had to run, that she and Danica's father were heading out to buy a new patio set, and Danica didn't feel the usual emptiness when the call ended. She'd develop a relationship with her mother on her terms, not her mother's. If it made Danica feel good to speak to her mom once a week, then her mother was just going to have to get used to being called often.

"Okay, we're ready," Candace said. Brandy was in her arms, wearing another of the outfits Danica had sent recently when her sister still lived in LA, an adorable sparkly purple tutu over tights. "I figure we'll be back by tenish, and my first interview is at noon. You're still okay to babysit?"

"Absolutely."

"You're the best, Danica. Coming home was the smartest thing I ever did."

Danica beamed and gave her sister a hug, and they headed out.

"Oh, and Danica? I know you may not believe it

right now, but Ford will be back. I know that like I know you. And I've gotten to know you very well."

"Well, I won't hope too hard on that one. But since I'm not gonna get over him for a long, long time, I might as well fantasize that he'll come bursting through the door to tell me he's been an idiot."

Candace smiled. "He will. Want to know how I know? Ford is not an idiot. That's very clear. So how long can he act like one before coming to his senses?"

Danica laughed, but she was a second away from crying. She wished she had her sister's faith, but after last night, she was out of hope where Ford Dawson was concerned.

Ford was back in his private spot at the Dawson Family Guest Ranch, through the brush and on the short path that led to the river, where he was sure there would be no guests. He'd gotten up way too early, jogged his miles, drank too much coffee, did two loads of laundry and he still had two hours before he had to be at work. He'd barely slept, waking up constantly, thinking about what he'd said to Danica, hating himself for hurting her but unable to move past this point he was stuck in.

Stuck. He'd thought moving home was going to

be about a fresh start, and instead he'd been pulled back into a time warp.

He heard footsteps and scowled, wondering how a guest had unearthed this perfect patch of solitude. The footsteps were coming closer. Dammit. Ford shot up, preparing to leave, but the face that greeted him was his brother, Zeke, a baby carrier on his chest, a pink-capped baby's head visible.

"Hey, this is our secret getaway," Zeke said with a grin.

"It *was* mine."

"Did you used to come here when we were kids? It was the best place to hide. No one ever found me during hide-and-seek."

Ford laughed. "I wouldn't even have thought to look here because I was under the false impression that no one knew it existed but me. That brush at the start looks really thick and wild."

"I have no doubt we all come here and have for decades," Zeke said.

"Lucy asleep?" he asked, gesturing at the baby.

"Yup. We're supposed to be spending the day together but here she is, dead to the world. Some father-daughter day," he said on a laugh.

"How'd you get to this point?" Ford asked. "How did any of you become so comfortable with fatherhood?"

"Well, to be honest, most of us fell for women with babies. So we had to or else."

Ford thought about that. "That damned diary really did a number on me. I can't shake it. I can know all I want that I can be a great dad and husband, but every time I think about either, I think about my mother's entries, and I just can't get past it. It's made me not want any part of a future with anyone. Particularly children."

"So you're just going to let Danica move on to someone else? The love of your life?"

"I already told her to move on. For all I know she's matched herself on a date with someone who's ready to get married and have kids."

"You know, Ford, it took me a while to get Dad and everything we went through out of my head and away from my relationship with Molly. I also thought I didn't want kids. But there comes a point where something forces the issue. And choosing nothing over everything is really dumb, bro. Dad is gone. Your mother is gone. The past is gone. You want to spend the next five years alone, stewing over a bad marriage that had nothing to do with you?"

"No, I don't. But I can't seem to get past it. That's the problem."

"But that problem is you, Ford. You've always

been our hero. We know where those little match-box cars came from on our birthdays every year, supposedly from Dad. We know where the bagged lunches came from when he told us to scram from the house for the days we were visiting. The kid, the teenager, who looked out for his five younger siblings isn't looking out for himself? That's hard to swallow."

Ford gave something of a shrug. "You know why I left Bear Ridge, Zeke. I have the same feeling of dread."

"I do know why you left. Because you were afraid you'd have to arrest your own father. And he baited you to do it at least twice—I was there one time, so I know. But Ford, like I just said, Dad is gone. The past is over. And Danica is here. A happy future is here. The five of us did it and if any of us could, it's you."

"Great, now I feel like I'm falling down in my siblings' estimation." He leaned his head back and let out a harsh breath.

"Never, Ford. Never. I get it. I'm just saying you're stronger than this."

Ford looked at Zeke, and he would have pulled him in for a hug if the baby wasn't in the way. He didn't feel stronger than the swirl of leaves moving in the April breeze.

"Don't give up happiness for bad memories," Zeke said. "That would be the worst thing you could do."

"I'd better get to the PD," Ford said.

"Ah, classic deflection. A business tactic I'm well used to."

"Nah, I really am due there. But I'll promise you that I'll think about what you said. You had some pretty intense points."

"But more importantly, I'm *right*."

Ford grinned and headed through the brush, his mind echoing with all his brother had said.

Breakfast with Junie had been wonderful. She'd been terrific with baby Brandy, and she and Candace had connected easily. They hadn't talked about their mom or the rest of the family; they were forging their own bonds, their own relationships. Junie had made an excuse for them to leave after an hour, and Danica knew her cousin needed to go slowly, that too much too soon would feel invasive after decades of nothing. They made a plan to get together every week, and Junie was looking forward to getting to know Trudy, who was close to her age. Now, as Danica got ready for work in her bedroom, she felt so hopeful about the future where her family was concerned.

She was slipping into her favorite four-inch tweed pumps when Candace burst into her room, waving what looked like a matchmaking form.

"I know you probably don't want to even think about dating, but I got curious about the match-making requests so was nosing through and I think I found the perfect guy for you." She held up the profile, and Danica recognized a dentist she'd dated already, back before she met Ford.

"Yup, we went out already. He talked nonstop about his ex-girlfriend and asked if I'd ever consid-ered breast implants. The date lasted twelve min-utes before I feigned a headache. No, wait, I didn't even have to fake it—he gave me one."

Candace offered a gentle smile. "That's the problem—so many people sound great on paper, but a list of traits mean nothing till you meet."

"Anyway, like you said, I won't be dating for a while. I'm content to just put couples together. Mayor Abbot told me I'm responsible for three engagements."

Her sister sat on the edge of her bed. "You look so sad, Dani. Is there anything I can do? I thought I'd try cheer and possibilities, but what you really need is time and hugs and old movies. Don't think I'm one of those women who ditches her sister for her boyfriend, either. If you want a movie night or to go to Prairie City and shop and just get away from Bear Ridge, I'm there. Anytime."

Danica leaned over and pulled Candace into a hug. "I love you."

"I love you, too." She looked at Danica, biting her lip. "What can I do for you today? I've got my interview at noon but after we can go for the soup and sandwich combo at the diner for lunch and then mani-pedis?"

"Lunch today is a work birthday party, but I appreciate it, Candace. And I will definitely take you up on those movie nights. You must be so excited for this afternoon's fun outing with Jasper and Brandy."

Her sister's eyes lit up. "I feel really hopeful about everything. I'm pretty crazy about Jasper Fields."

Danica smiled. "It's the best feeling in the world. To be in love." Even if hurts like hell, she added silently.

Her sister seemed to pick that up. "I didn't think Ford Dawson was an idiot, but he must be," Candace said. "Just a matter of time before the right guy makes his way into your life. And then it'll be too late for Ford."

"Yeah," Danica agreed, but she could hardly believe that. Who could top Ford? Who could she love more than she loved him? She was never sure about the concept of a soul mate, that there was one person who was *your person*. But Ford was that for her. And she believed she was that for him.

"Sorry, this is hardly making you feel better. Want me to bring you some coffee?"

"Yes, actually. Thanks, Candace."

Candace gave Danica a gentle pat on her arm and then left the room.

She might not have the man she loved, but she did have her sister.

Ford had just gotten back in his car at the ranch gatehouse when his cell phone rang. Junie Maywood. He'd programmed it in a year and half ago when he'd first gone to see her about the map and the diary.

"Hi, Junie," he said, wondering what this could be about.

"I can't talk long because I'm about to do major spring cleaning of my house now that I'll be having company on a regular basis. I never have people over, and now I'm suddenly a hostess with company yesterday and this morning."

He could hear the happiness in her voice. "I know Danica was looking forward to coming over with her sister and the baby for breakfast," he said.

He'd learned long ago not to rush people in talking; they would when they were ready and then they'd really let loose. In his line of work, he needed motor mouths.

"Listen, I couldn't say anything with Danica over since I don't know what's between you two," she said, "but I wanted to tell you something your mother said. A few years after she left your father and you two were more settled."

He took a deep breath, not sure what he was about to hear.

"She was over helping me weed, and you were running around with the dog, not the ones I have now, of course. And she looked at you and she said, 'Junie, you know what my deepest wish is for Ford?' And I said, 'No, what?' And she said, 'For him to have a beautiful love story. To find the right person for the right reasons.' Isn't that lovely? And then she added something I'll never forget. She said, 'Bo and I set a terrible example for him, but he's going to steer the family ship in a different direction. To all good things.' She was so happy when she said all that. Like she was setting your course by putting it out there."

He sat down hard on the kitchen chair, his mother's words echoing in his head, entering his heart. He could feel them seeping inside his chest. *Steer the family ship in a different direction.*

His siblings had done that.

To find the right person for the right reasons.

He thought about the diary, the torn-up page. His mother had known she'd planned to stay with Bo for the wrong reasons. But she'd come out of that marriage still believing in love, in change— for herself. And she had changed her life.

Why hadn't he realized that before? She'd gone back to school. She'd gotten a decent-paying job, and she'd raised Ford with all the good things she'd wanted instilled in him. She'd stayed in town so that he'd have easy access to his dad, despite how terrible their marriage had been. She'd made him what he was with her strength and her big heart.

Man, had he been an idiot.

"I appreciate you telling me all this, Junie. Now *this* was something I needed to know."

"Well, I'd better get to dusting for the next visit," Junie said. "Bye now."

There was a click, and he smiled. *I owe you one, Junie Maywood*, he thought, mentally adding two things to his to-do list after work.

He just hoped he wouldn't be too late.

Chapter Eighteen

Danica glanced at her phone—5:32 p.m. She sat on the patio in the backyard, a glass of white wine on the table, a bowl of pistachios beside it. The late afternoon was gorgeous and warm, low sixties, the sun still out, and she stretched out on her zero-gravity chair, taking a sip of her wine. Everything inside hurt like hell, but life around her was good and solid and kept her positive.

Candace was still out with Jasper and Brandy and would be till around seven. They'd gone to the petting zoo and then to Prairie City. Candace had texted her photos of the adorable classic teddy bear Jasper had bought for Brandy. Danica immediately envisioned her niece at nine, at fifteen, her teddy bear from Daddy beside her. Yes, she was getting way ahead of herself, but the picture felt true. She could see Candace and Jasper getting married at Christmastime, Brandy toddling down the aisle.

She reached for her folder of matchmaking forms—Mayor Abbott had heaped a new batch on her, now that the crimes-of-vengeance perpetrators had decided to focus on love. The speed dating event was back on for this weekend and she'd need a new partner to help with that and the forms.

A new partner. She didn't want a new anything. She just wanted Ford.

Her phone pinged and she glanced at it, expecting it to be Pauline Abbott to ask if she could drop off more matchmaking requests.

But it was Ford.

He texted: Can we talk face-to-face? Right now?

Don't get your hopes up, she thought. Maybe he's just coming to say he wants to be friends and plans to honor his commitment to the matchmaking and speed dating.

I'm out back, she texted.

He responded: Be there in five.

She took another sip of wine, and suddenly there he was, still in uniform. He looked so gorgeous under the setting sun.

"Junie called me this morning with another story," he said, sitting down on the chair across from hers. "About my mother's hopes for me. That I'd steer the family ship in a new direction—to all good things."

Danica sat up straight. He was not here about matchmaking or speed dating.

"You're all good things, Danica. The diary tore me up, but my mother's words about finding the right person for the right reasons—got right in here," he said, bringing a fist to his chest. "You're the right person for the right reasons. You always were."

Tears stung her eyes and she was too overcome to speak for a moment. She leaned forward and took his hands. "First I ran from you and then you ran from me, and now here we are."

"Here we are." He got down on one knee and took a small velvet box out of his pocket and opened it. A beautiful antique diamond ring twinkled. "I don't want to wait another second to start my life with you, Danica. I love you. Children, no children—all I want is you."

"All I want is you. But I'd like two kids." She stared down at the ring, then at him.

"Will you marry me?" he asked.

She flew into his arms. "Yes. Yes, yes, yes."

He held her tight and kissed her. "We made our own match, after all."

Danica grinned, kissing her fiancé again. Theirs would be a match to last forever.

Epilogue

Just a few days before Christmas, there was a double wedding in the biggest ballroom at the Dawson Family Guest Ranch lodge. Danica and Candace, the two brides, were in the small bridal room putting on finishing touches. They'd covered the something old, the something new and the something blue, but they both realized they'd forgotten "something borrowed."

Danica was about to call Molly to ask for the beautiful gold bangle she wore every day; it had been a gift from Danica for her eighteenth birthday, and Danica liked the idea of borrowing something she'd given her best friend so long ago.

Candace got out her phone to ask Aunt Trudy if she could bring over Brandy's jeweled baby barrette; she planned to put it in her own hair, which sounded very sweet to Danica.

But a knock sounded at the door, and Judith Dunbar came in. The sisters had fully expected their parents to come to the wedding; even Judith couldn't have made an excuse for something so special—the double wedding of her daughters. Over the past several months, Danica and Candace had made weekly calls to their parents, and though it had taken Judith a while to warm up and open up, she had quite a bit. She'd been touched that Danica had asked her to play the wedding march for their trek down the aisle, Judith was a very talented pianist.

Judith was wearing a beautiful pale blue gown, her blond hair in a shiny bob. "I have something for both of you." She reached into her little beaded purse and pulled out two pairs of diamond stud earrings. "These were my mother's and I'd love it if you wore them. Unless you have your heart set on earrings already."

Danica glanced at Candace and smiled.

"Mom, I was about to borrow my baby daughter's rhinestone barrette to have something borrowed, so you saved me from baby wear."

Judith laughed and handed each of her daughters the earrings.

Danica put hers on and admired how they twinkled in the mirror. "I feel like Nana is here with us now."

Judith hugged each of them and then left, her eyes misty.

"Wonders will never cease," Candace said, turning left and right to see her sparkling earlobes. "Was that our mother?"

"Everything is so different. We wanted it to be and so it is."

Candace seemed to think about that for a second. "You're right. We're both marrying the men we love. I'm getting my degree in early childhood education. You're taking classes in interior design. Our mother and her cousin are both actually in the same room at the same time and not killing each other."

Their mother wasn't thrilled that her daughters had gotten close with Junie, but she'd accepted it. The cousins had been forced into the same room twice in the past several months for wedding festivities, and though they got along like oil and water, there they both were—for family. And that was family for you.

Danica smiled. "Here's to us," she said, lifting the two glasses of champagne that Molly had brought in earlier. They each took a sip and then immediately fixed their lipstick.

Danica peered out the door into the ballroom, which was full of guests who were mingling over champagne. All the Dawsons were there—Noah, Sara, and their year-old twins Annabel and Chance; Daisy, Harrison, and their baby Tony; Axel, Sadie, their toddler Danny and their baby Jasmine; Rex, Maisey and one-year-old Chloe; and Zeke, Molly and little Lucy. What no one knew, except for Danica and Ford, was that another little Dawson was about to join the family, helping to steer the family ship into new directions. She was pregnant, just six weeks at this point, and she and Ford were keeping that under wraps until she was out of the first trimester. Danica had never known she could feel this happy, this excited, this full of hope. She was going to have a baby.

As a lovely classical piece of music began—Judith on piano—the guests began moving to their seats and Danica and Candace's father came over in his tuxedo, all smiles. Their dad was a quiet person, but they could both see how touched he was to have been asked to escort his daughters down the aisle.

As she wrapped her arm around her father's, Candace on the other side of him, she looked down the aisle at her waiting groom, and his expression almost made her cry. He looked so happy, so handsome.

She made her way down the red carpet, her gaze on Ford, the two of them the only people who knew that their baby-to-be was attending their parents' wedding. A brand-new family was forming, a new beginning forged.

* * * * *

Don't miss Melissa Senate's next book,
part of the Montana Mavericks:
The Real Cowboys of Bronco Heights continuity,
available September 2021.

And in the meantime, check out these other
emotional Western themed romances:

The Rancher's Promise
By Brenda Harlen

She Dreamed of a Cowboy
By Joanna Sims

Making Room for the Rancher
By Christy Jeffries

Available now wherever
Harlequin Special Edition
books and ebooks are sold!

COMING NEXT MONTH FROM

Ⓗ HARLEQUIN

SPECIAL EDITION

#2833 BEFORE SUMMER ENDS
by Susan Mallery

Nissa Lang knows Desmond Stilling is out of her league. He's a CEO, she's a teacher. He's gorgeous, she's...not. So when her house-sitting gig falls through and Desmond offers her a place to stay for the summer, she vows not to reveal how she's felt about him since their first—and only—kiss.

#2834 THE LAST ONE HOME
The Bravos of Valentine Bay • by Christine Rimmer

Ian McNeill has returned to Valentine Bay to meet the biological family he can't remember. Along for the ride is his longtime best friend, single mom Ella Haralson. Will this unexpected reunion turn Ian into a family man in more ways than one?

#2835 AN OFFICER AND A FORTUNE
The Fortunes of Texas: The Hotel Fortune • by Nina Crespo

Captain Collin Waldon is on leave from the military, tending to his ailing father. He's not looking for romantic entanglements—*especially* not with Nicole Fortune, the executive chef of Roja Restaurant in the struggling Hotel Fortune. Yet these two unlikely lovers seem perfect for each other, until Collin's reassignment threatens their newfound bliss...

#2836 THE TWIN PROPOSAL
Lockharts Lost & Found • by Cathy Gillen Thacker

Mackenzie Lockhart just proposed to Griff Montgomery, her best bud since they were kids in foster care. Once Griff gets his well-deserved promotion, they can return to their independent lives. But when they cross the line from friends to lovers, there's no going back. With twins on the way, is this their chance to turn a temporary arrangement into a can't-lose formula for love?

#2837 THE MARINE'S BABY BLUES
The Camdens of Montana • by Victoria Pade

Tanner Camden never thought he'd end up getting a call that he might be a father—or that his ex had died, leaving little Poppy in the care of her sister, Addie Markham. Addie may have always resented him, but with their shared goal of caring for Poppy, they're willing to set aside their differences. Even if allowing their new feelings to bloom means both of them could get hurt when the paternity test results come back...

#2838 THE RANCHER'S FOREVER FAMILY
Texas Cowboys & K-9s • by Sasha Summers

Sergeant Hayden Mitchell's mission—give every canine veteran the perfect forever home. But when it comes to Sierra, a sweet Labrador, Hayden isn't sure Lizzie Vega fits the bill. When a storm leaves her stranded at his ranch, the hardened former military man wonders if Lizzie is the perfect match for Sierra...and him...

**YOU CAN FIND MORE INFORMATION ON UPCOMING HARLEQUIN TITLES,
FREE EXCERPTS AND MORE AT HARLEQUIN.COM.**

HSECNM0421

Nissa Lang knows Desmond Stilling is out of her league.
He's a CEO, she's a teacher. He's gorgeous, she's…
not. So when her house-sitting gig falls through and
Desmond offers her a place to stay for the summer, she
vows not to reveal how she's felt about him since their
first—and only—kiss.

Read on for a sneak peek at
Before Summer Ends,
by #1 New York Times *bestselling author*
Susan Mallery.

"You're welcome to join me if you'd like. Unless you
have plans. It's Saturday, after all."

Plans as in a date? Yeah, not so much these days. In
fact, she hadn't been in a serious relationship since she
and James had broken up over two years ago.

"I don't date," she blurted before she could stop
herself. "I mean, I can, but I don't. Or I haven't been.
Um, lately."

She consciously pressed her lips together to stop
herself from babbling like an idiot, despite the fact that
the damage was done.

"So, dinner?" Desmond asked, rescuing her without
commenting on her babbling.

"I'd like that. After I shower. Meet back down here in half an hour?"

"Perfect."

There was an awkward moment when they both tried to go through the kitchen door at the same time. Desmond stepped back and waved her in front of him. She hurried out, then raced up the stairs and practically ran for her bedroom. Once there, she closed the door and leaned against it.

"Talking isn't hard," she whispered to herself. "You've been doing it since you were two. You know how to do this."

But when it came to being around Desmond, knowing and doing were two different things.

Don't miss
Before Summer Ends *by Susan Mallery,*
available May 2021 wherever
Harlequin Special Edition books and ebooks are sold.

Harlequin.com

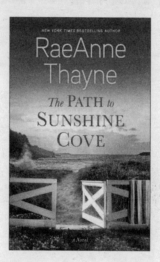